The Beginning Comes Quietly

by

Susan JP Owens

The Dawning Series

This is a work of fiction. Names, characters, places, and incidents are either the product of the author's imagination or are used fictitiously, and any resemblance to actual persons living or dead, business establishments, events, or locales, is entirely coincidental.

The Beginning Comes Quietly

Cover Art by *Diana Carlile*

The Wild Rose Press, Inc.
PO Box 708
Adams Basin, NY 14410-0708
Visit us at www.thewildrosepress.com

Publishing History
First Faery Rose Edition, 2014
Digital ISBN 978-1-62830-490-9
Print ISBN 978-1-5092-1476-1

The Dawning Series
Published in the United States of America

Tingles danced from the nape of her neck, traveling down both arms to her fingertips. The familiar signal changed to a pulsing rhythmic beat. Accustomed to the trigger, she rested her forehead on the steering wheel, closed her eyes, and gathered strength to persevere what was coming.

He wanted her to witness another murder. The assailant fed on the victim's fear. Peyton's muscles clenched. Sweat beaded on her upper lip while perspiration trickled down her temples.

A man wearing black—she could only make out an outline, never the features—ripped open the woman's chest with a serrated butcher knife.

Pain sliced through her. The coppery smell of blood filtered to her nostrils.

The victim's skin splayed, exposing tissue and bone. The killer's arm arced. The final strike slit the woman's throat, nearly decapitating her.

Peyton clapped a palm over her mouth to keep from hurling.

Lights dimmed as if signaling the conclusion of a one-act tragedy, then a curtain of darkness enveloped her mind. Despair and revulsion roiled in her gut. Incapable of movement, she was unable to defend or help, and the helplessness tore her apart. Even her psyche splintered into tiny pieces, too small to put back together. Maybe she was crazy after all.

Dedication

To my hero and husband, Jimmy,
thank you for your enduring love and support, my
gratitude to my sisters and brother for their continued
encouragement and Rogan Ranly for giving me terrific
character names. God Bless you all.

Chapter One

Peyton Adams slid the gearshift into park and exhaled. The air ruffled her hair then settled, tickling her face. The drive to get to her best friend's mountain home and guest cabins had been intense. She'd taken the back routes which added to the long journey and the snow-covered roads were dangerous. As if the treacherous highways weren't a big enough concern, with Peyton's problems that dragged her into the depths of hell, she thanked her lucky stars she made it in one piece.

How could she begin to explain what was happening to her, when she didn't fully understand? The beginning came quietly, one death at a time. The rapid mental images rifling through her mind was like a horrible dream, but the nightmares happened during the day when she was fully awake. What sane person would believe this could really happen? Now, the unbearable agony debilitated her to the point of incapacitation.

There were two reasons for coming here. Jillian had an amazing gift and Peyton would need her friend's healing hand with the headaches that always accompanied the attacks. Plus, she accepted a deadline to finish a screen adaptation for one of her books by Valentine's Day.

She inhaled a cleansing breath, releasing it between

thinned lips. "Think you can complete this project in eight weeks? Maybe next time, you won't let your mouth overload your ass."

Tingles danced from the nape of her neck, traveling down both arms to her fingertips. The familiar signal changed to a pulsing rhythmic beat. Accustomed to the trigger, she rested her forehead on the steering wheel, closed her eyes, and gathered strength to persevere what was coming.

He wanted her to witness another murder. The assailant fed on the victim's fear. Peyton's muscles clenched. Sweat beaded on her upper lip while perspiration trickled down her temples.

A man wearing black—she could only make out an outline, never the features—ripped open the woman's chest with a serrated butcher knife.

Pain sliced through her. The coppery smell of blood filtered to her nostrils.

The victim's skin splayed, exposing tissue and bone. The killer's arm arced. The final strike slit the woman's throat nearly decapitating her.

Peyton clapped a palm over her mouth to keep from hurling.

Lights dimmed as if signaling the conclusion of a one act tragedy, then a curtain of darkness enveloped her mind. Despair and revulsion roiled in her gut. Incapable of movement, she was unable to defend or help, and the helplessness tore her apart. Even her psyche splintered into tiny pieces, too small to put back together. Maybe she was crazy after all.

Peyton blinked. Her breathing slowed. She swallowed the lump in her throat, taking the acidic taste with it. In the past, she'd only observed the killings by the demented psycho. Initially, Peyton thought she was hallucinating, but the national news convinced her otherwise. She straightened in her seat and checked her chest and throat for gashes or a puncture wound. Zilch. After a year of remaining a powerless bystander, this was the first time she experienced the victim's pain. She sighed. Relief flowed from her head to her feet that the woman didn't suffer for very long.

Nausea churned in her stomach like a smoldering cauldron of an evil brew. The attacker's concoction prepared exclusively for Peyton simmered and fermented not only in her mind, but this time he claimed and controlled her body, and with each occurrence, his power grew.

There was good news, if she could call it that. At least the killer didn't torture this lady like he had the others.

Damn, had she lost her mind? Comparing the deaths of each woman and ranking them on a scale of cruelty was beyond sick. Call it intuition, but she understood that the man, an executioner in every sense of the word and a spawn of Satan, would kill her before she had any answers. Peyton shook her head to dispel the premonition.

Her tummy lurched. She'd eventually be his target, and that frightened and irritated her with matching intensity. The realization she'd die an excruciating death by his hands terrified her, and the fact she was at his mercy for the timing aggravated the hell out of her. Her emotions fluctuated with severe ups and downs never fully balancing. One moment, she'd have a positive outlook, and the next, he had her figuratively tied in knots.

Her blurry vision cleared and her heart palpitations slowed to normal. Peering through the windshield, the Montana sky cast an eerie bluish-gray and the tumultuous clouds swirled. She shivered. Usually, she enjoyed the stroke of colors from nature's pallet, but this was too close to her turmoil. According to the weather report, the heavy overcast would turn into the biggest snowstorm of the century across the area. Good thing she didn't have to leave any time soon.

The Southerland's majestic estate stood before her. Jillian and Richard loved this part of the country. Their home was always warm and welcoming on the inside, the very thing she needed right now. She glanced in the rearview mirror. Their stables, barns, and outbuildings nestled in the valley next to the river resembled a winter oil painting on a Christmas card. The only thing missing was a cardinal perched on a branch of an evergreen. Like a spider web, roads splintered off the expanse of the circular drive leading to private cabins for guests. She hadn't been here in a long time and looked forward to the isolation, quiet, and the healing Jillian gave her.

Her gaze caught Jill and her best friend's brother descending the cleared steps. Her breath hitched. Why she still loved her ex-fiancé, who ended their relationship, she'd never understand. If she'd known Cole was visiting, she would've made other plans. But she was here, and she needed Jillian. She would just have to keep her distance from him.

Somehow Jill's presence alleviated the headaches and downtime after these episodes. Peyton climbed out of the vehicle, closed the door, and waited for her friend, purposely averting her eyes away from Cole.

4

Jillian wrapped her arms around Peyton's shoulders and gave her a bear hug. "I'm so glad you came."

Peyton drew on Jill's energy, allowing Jilly to mend her broken mind and heal the searing hurt in her body. "So am I."

"Are you okay, now?" Jillian whispered. Jill knew about Peyton's secret but didn't consider her a freak. Peyton understood her experiences were unusual. Hell, they were freaking bizarre. No one should have to endure this crap.

Peyton nodded. "Thanks, I don't know how you fix me."

Jilly released her, and Peyton ached with the lost sensation of her therapeutic touch. The only thing her best friend couldn't give her was peace. Peyton doubted if she would experience serenity ever again.

Jill patted Peyton's arm. "I'm glad you came. I tried to get Leah to visit, but she declined."

"How is your sister doing?"

"Good, she's in Louisiana elbow deep in research. Her cryptic voice mail gave me the creeps. She said something about sensing a need to look into a few things."

Peyton wanted to ask more, but thought better of it. "Tell her I said hello next time you talk to her. Where do I—?"

"I've put you in number three, knowing you'd like privacy. You'll love it. The lake is beautiful this time of year. When the sun comes up, the light reflects off the snow and ice. Cole can help with your bags."

Peyton nodded at her ex-fiancé.

He grunted and jammed his hands in the hip-length, leather jacket. His mouth slightly curled up at each end and the familiar affection from his gaze tugged at her heart. Peyton surreptitiously scanned Cole's onyx five-o-clock shadow covering his square jaw. She yearned for his whiskers to rasp across her skin at the one place no one had been since him. His eyes traveled from the top of her head down to her toes, and her libido danced with delight. She mentally kicked herself. *Remember. He was the one that left without an explanation.*

"I don't need your help." Peyton turned her back on Cole to discourage him from taking his sister's advice and lend a hand. She straightened her spine determined not to succumb to her hidden desires and squelch the lust blazing into a firestorm. She'd made the mistake of giving her love to Jillian's brother once and she would never give him or anyone else the opportunity to break her heart again. As far as she was concerned, successful relationships were for others, like Jill and her husband, Richard. Besides, she had more pressing problems to deal with. "Just point in the general direction, I'll find it."

"Sure." Jillian pointed. "Take that road, and you'll see My Heart's Desire on the right. Cole, would you help Peyton get settled?"

When Cole stepped forward, Peyton conveyed her best go-to-hell look. "Don't bother."

His ice-blue sweater underneath the black coat zipped halfway matched his eyes which wreaked havoc inside her. Desire journeyed low and settled between her thighs. She shook off the erotic sensations. Damn her insipid propensities for wanting his touch. She assumed she had destroyed her weakness years ago, three to be exact.

"I don't mind." Cole advanced another pace.

"If you're not busy, maybe, we can have coffee in the morning." Peyton ignored Cole and waited for Jill's answer.

"We're having dinner in the main dining room at seven tonight. Please join us. Richard wants to visit with everyone. It's been ages since we've seen you. I promise I won't bother you again until our coffee date."

"You never eat in the formal area, what's the occasion?" Peyton inched closer to Jill and further from Cole.

"You, Cole, Christmas, New Year's. I love this time of year."

"I know you do." Peyton smiled. "I'll see you then."

The drive to her residence for the next two months mellowed her jumpy nerves. Between the vision and seeing her ex-fiancé, she was rattled. Cole had the power to draw her in. One of many reasons why she'd made sure there were at least a thousand miles in between them. Since he was staying at the main house, she'd have to settle for a steep hill and one long valley. As for the mental images, she'd rather not think about it and made an extra effort to erase the malicious memories.

She stopped the car in front of the cabin and hopped out. The pathway leading to the front porch had been plowed. The blown snow piled high on each side drew her gaze to the entrance decorated with a beautiful wreath. The tips of the red velvet bow adornment flapped from the brisk breeze. It was these moments of life and tranquility she held onto, not the red carpet rides. Granted, accepting awards were awesome and thrilling, but the snapshots of her existence comingling with nature truly humbled her enough to remember she was on this earth for a brief period of time. She sighed and shook off the sentimental thoughts. Snuggled in those reflections was a key word. Brief.

Peyton grabbed her bags from the backseat and headed toward the door. Snow crunched under her feet as she followed the sidewalk carefully traversing up the three steps to a wide porch. Wood lay stacked against the one story stone structure. A glow emanated from the windows carrying the burnt offering of a warm fire. She smiled at Jillian and Richard's thoughtfulness.

The whine of an engine thundered behind her. She whirled toward the sound. An ATV skidded to a stop. Long male legs straddled the seat, then they hefted from the vehicle.

"Cole?"

"Were you expecting someone else?"

"I wasn't expecting anyone including you." Cole threw her equilibrium off. He had the innate ability to cause and capture every passionate thread in her and just as quickly, with one word or look, unravel the tightly woven fibers of her balance and sanity. What little she had left.

Disgusted with herself, she pivoted to open the front door and slipped. Her feet skated in different directions. She stretched to grab the door handle. Her bags fell from her grasp. Some of the contents in her purse spilled, slid across the slick flagstone, dropping off the veranda one by one into the holly bushes.

The expletives on her lips begged to escape. Instead, she clamped her mouth shut. She picked up her handbag, stalked down the steps. She lowered to her knees and stretched her arm through the prickly plants to retrieve her things. "Ouch." Trying like hell not to be jabbed again, she scooped up her brush, lipstick and the other personal items in one hand, then brushed the snow off before she placed them back in her purse. This was taking too long with Cole hovering over her backside.

"Let me help." The sexy, bass timbre of Cole's voice set fire to the dark lust she had put a damper on since he walked out of her life.

"No need."

He chuckled. "Still an accident waiting to happen."

The comment didn't deserve an answer nor would she give one. The comb was the only thing remaining. She gathered it from beneath the sculpted landscape and straightened right into a hard wall. Cole's chest.

He grasped both shoulders and spun her. His lips thinned and his brows furrowed. "What are you doing here?"

She tilted her head and viewed the man who towered over her by seven inches. "Like it's any of your business."

He snarled, and his finger pointed to her then him. "I think we're Jilly's victims." His hands dropped to his side. "At first, I thought you were behind this. But when you first saw me. I'm betting you didn't have a clue either."

She inched toward the cabin, gaining more distance from Cole. The heat from his body permeated her coat and clothing, sizzling to her flesh. All Cole ever had to do was stand near her and erotic passion spiraled out of control, especially when he talked. This time wasn't any different. "I need to get ready for dinner." She opened the door, crossed the threshold, and slammed the door shut.

****

After the dinner of grilled trout and vegetables, the personal chef ended the feast with a Flaming Alaskan desert.

Peyton swallowed the last remnant of the sweet decadent reward she allowed herself to have during the holidays. "I'll need to add extra exercises to my workout."

Jill lowered her coffee cup on the saucer. "You're welcome to use the gym and inside pool."

"When's a good time?"

"Our trainers are on vacation so we are too." Jillian waggled her eyebrows. "Although, Richard and I do get our exercise—"

"Jill, too much information." Richard rose. "Let's have a brandy in the library."

Richard winked at Jilly then scooted Peyton's chair away from the rectangular table. "Ready?" He tucked Peyton's hand in the crook of his arm. "If I hadn't stopped her..."

Peyton nodded. "Don't be embarrassed. Jill loves you and she feels comfortable enough to share with us her most intimate thoughts."

"I know. You'd think I'd be used to it by now." Richard smiled and guided her to a room of mahogany wood and rich, textured fabrics. The interior decorating had Jillian's hand written all over it, masculine for her husband, yet the design carried a palatial flair and warmth for family and friends. The balance was extraordinary.

Cole escorted his sister and offered Jillian the

empty chair beside Peyton. When he wanted to, Cole could be a gentleman. One of the many traits she had fallen in love with.

After Richard filled the snifters, Cole passed one to her and one to Jill. Cole returned to sit by Richard at the opposite corner while she and Jillian shared the warmth of the fireplace.

Jillian swirled the liquor in her goblet. The amber liquid reflected the flames. "I hope you're not angry with me. I'm not giving up hope that you'll be my sister-in-law. Although, I think my intervention might be too late."

Jill's heartfelt apology rang true. How could Peyton resent Jilly when she would've loved to have her as a sister? "I could never be mad at you. Besides, I'm over Cole." Yeah, she'd lie to keep Jillian from feeling bad.

"You must be or you would still have on the bracelet Cole gave to you." Jillian focused on her bare wrist.

"I lost it at the convention in New Orleans about a year ago." Peyton rubbed the flesh she refused to adorn since then.

"You're still having visions."

Jill wasn't asking. Peyton exhaled a lengthy breath. "How many?"

"I've only had one today. So this is a good day." Peyton laced her fingers together and placed her hands on her lap. She held back they were getting worse with every episode to keep Jillian from worrying.

"Does Cole know you have a gift?"

"A gift? Never thought of it that way." Jillian always saw the glass half-full. She was not naive but

11

grasped for the positive energy in the world. Peyton admired her best friend's characteristic, because without a doubt her own outlook was far different. She glanced over at the two men deep in conversation and shook her head. Her eyes trailed over Cole's broad shoulders, panning down his back to the trim waist. "This is the first time I've seen or talked to him since he broke off our engagement."

Peyton disconnected her gaze, set her glass on top of the etched stone coaster intricately carved with a deer surrounded by the mountains, and rose from the winged back chair. "I'm bushed and need some rest. Thank you for a wonderful evening." She kissed Jill's cheek and hugged her.

When she straightened, Richard stood beside her. He circled his arm around her shoulder and nestled her to his side. "You doing okay?"

Peyton lifted her chin in a silent answer and returned his brotherly affection with a quick embrace. "Thank you for everything. You and Jillian have been a Godsend to me."

Richard placed his hand on the small of her back. "I'm glad you're here. It's been too long. Let me get your coat and walk you to your car."

****

The hearth in Peyton's cabin burned a brilliant orange luminance as she cuddled on the couch in her extra-large warm ups and fluffy socks with non-skid bottoms. As predicted, the snowstorm hit an hour ago. She cradled the cup of hot cocoa, warming her fingers. The hypnotizing blaze soothed her frayed nerves from Cole's presence at the dinner table. She was amazed at how strong she'd been to put up the walls of indifference toward Cole.

She reflected back to when she'd met him. The attorney from a prominent law firm she'd used frequently invited her to their Christmas cocktail party. She didn't have time for dating and flew solo. Cole had been a junior partner and the multitude of women hitting on him during the social staggered her imagination. She'd resisted his overtures for the better part of six months, but his persistence broke through her defenses, leading to their first date. A year later, he'd asked her to marry him. She'd been on top of the world and ready to start a family.

Within several months, their connection died, something had gone horribly wrong, but she couldn't point to a particular reason. Originally, she placed the blame with Cole's work, except that wasn't the answer. He'd become aloof and with the widening distance between them the vast void grew until her universe collapsed into a black hole.

Now, Cole's last name appeared first in the firm's string of attorney's surnames, their wrecked relationship a fatality to his rise of fame and fortune. If only...those words were useless and she'd best remember her mantra, *survival, just survive the next twenty-four hours.*

She had other problems to deal with besides dissecting why Cole acted the way he did. She didn't know how to overcome Satan's spawn's attacks or when he would strike again. Was she losing grip on reality? The question haunted her on a daily basis. Either way didn't bode well. As long as the killer had control over her, she refused to date, let alone build an attachment with any man. She couldn't allow anyone to be a part of her life. It was too dangerous.

A knock catapulted her out of her revelry. She placed the mug on the end table. "Come in." Maybe she shouldn't have said that without checking who was on the other side. She held her breath.

The cold whoosh of air carried the snowflakes inside and dotted Cole's black hair. He closed the door and shook his head, flinging the icy crystals in a three-foot circumference while stomping his feet on the thick entrance rug. His long ebony eyelashes heavy with remnants of the melted snow shimmered from the indirect light.

Cole's blue eyes gleamed like the proverbial wolf. "Thought I'd check and see how you're doing."

Her tummy quivered. One minute she despised him and the next, she wished he'd plunder her body. Heat infused between her legs, swelling in response to his presence and voice.

Cole's million dollar smile twisted into a sexy slant. Mental images crowded past her barricades, specifically the ones where his mouth had given her pleasure. She often wondered whether he gave every woman the same gratification or had he indulged only her with his wicked and wonderful tongue. She grudgingly acknowledged the former rather than the latter. "Why would you care?"

"Just trying to be neighborly." He shrugged.

The leather gloves he wore outlined his large hands. He tugged at the tips. Slowly, he peeled the material off of each digit, stripping his fingers naked. Cole's coat slid off with one deft movement, and he pivoted to hang it on the hall tree. The blue jeans encased his awesome ass, sinewy thighs and calves. He utilized the bootjack, taking off one boot then the other.

Cole strode to the fireplace in his stocking feet, rubbing his palms together. The height of stone base rose to his knees. He positioned his right foot on the flat hearth, cocked his hip, then braced an elbow on his thigh. Cole seemed mesmerized by the flickering flames. He shook his head as if releasing his thoughts and turned to face her. His brows furrowed in a straight line. This was the first time she'd ever seen him unsure of what to say.

Give him a courtroom, he'd parry and thrust his points with finesse. Most people never understood he'd stuck the foil through their heart until they were left bleeding and gasping for their last breath.

"Would you like a cup of coffee or hot chocolate?" Her voice wavered under his scrutiny.

"No. Richard stocks the bar." His lips curled into a smirk.

"Help yourself then." Uncomfortable with the warring emotions Cole provoked, Peyton snuggled into the sofa, tugging the homemade quilt around her shoulders.

"To answer the inquiry lingering in your mind, I usually stay here." The clink of ice dropping into a glass and the splash of liquid pouring intermingled with his whiskey voice.

"Oh." *Damn.* She cleared her throat and tried to relax.

"May I?" He indicated the end of the brown leather couch.

She drew her knees under her chin, scooting her rear against the far armrest. "By all means." His cologne and unique smell wafted past her nose, musky and all male.

He sipped the straight bourbon then gazed into her eyes. "What have you been up to?"

She hesitated. "Do you really want to know?"

He grimaced. "You always did answer with a question. I ask again."

"Not much, you?" She squirmed, tugging the blanket closer.

"You parlay well and deflected the subject to me. But, I don't give up."

Cole didn't chat just to have a conversation. His glacial eyes transformed once again into the carnivorous alpha male hunting for information. "Well?"

"Jillian invited me here so I could finish my work. You?"

"I'm taking some time off."

Cole never took a vacation day let alone an extended leave of absence. She softened her words. "What's wrong?"

He shrugged one shoulder. "Nothing, I wanted some R&R."

An uneasy air filled the room in the quiet seconds that followed. "If you ever want to talk, I'll listen."

Cole snorted. "I'm not that hard up."

Hurt slammed into her heart. "McLeod, you're such a prick."

"Glad to see I can still get a rise out of you, that's a good sign."

"You're an arrogant bastard. I'm going to bed. Let yourself out." She threw the quilt off, padded to her bedroom and slammed the door shut.

After two steps, tingles slithered down her arms,

rushing to her fingertips. The room swirled with a kaleidoscope of dark, menacing colors and images. Her heart pounded and shrieks hammered in her ears. "Oh God, not again." Peyton bowed her head.

Shivers escalated to tremors coursing through her extremities. Her legs gave out. She shoved her hands in front of her and softened her fall. "Ugh." The carpeting had helped a little, but pain shot from her knees and elbows while the imagery exploded in full color.

The attacker had a woman in a death grip. His fingers tightened around her neck, and his thumbs squeezed her windpipe. The victim needed air. The lady's eyes bulged then dulled.

Peyton struggled with the lethargy in her limbs. She tried to rip him away from the lifeless form, but she failed. Her lungs ached to release the sobs fighting to escape and to scream at the maniac for killing again.

He released the victim and spun toward Peyton. This was the first time she'd seen his face. She'd never forget his crazed eyes and pig nose. She drew her hands into fists and pummeled his chest. "You son-of-a-bitch."

The man sneered. "Soon, my sweet toy…soon."

His sinister laugh plunged through the walls of her strength, smashing the barrier into smithereens. Peyton choked. His breath stunk of Boudin sausage. She ceased struggling. All of her energy vanished. She slipped into darkness, letting the mystic sleep swallow her.

Chapter Two

Cole lowered to the floor, gathered Peyton, and cradled her in his embrace. Her eyes had glazed into a glassy pool of tears, then she passed out. He swept his knuckles across Peyton's cheek, wiping the beads of sweat from her clammy skin. She'd punched his ribs and he'd deflected several blows, but one nailed his right eye. He'd have a shiner by morning. What the hell happened to her?

He arranged Peyton's legs under one arm and wrapped the other around her shoulders. Peyton's petite body weighed next to nothing, she'd lost a considerable amount of weight since he'd last seen her. He rose and placed her on the tall, country-style bed. Peyton whimpered as he covered her with the homemade quilt. Retrieving a washcloth from the linen closet, he doused it with cold water and wiped the perspiration from her face and neck. He checked her pulse. What should've been a strong and steady beat was thready.

Peyton thrashed under the covers. The large warm ups she had on twisted around her neck and she gurgled.

"Damn it." He whisked the blankets off and untangled the material from her throat. Peyton gasped and inhaled a deep breath. "Not happening again." He undressed Peyton down to her silk camisole and lacy panties. The hot pink socks with the lime green polka dots had to go too.

He sat on the edge of the bed and sighed. Peyton had a lot of explaining to do when she woke. Would she disclose or hide her problems? Cole wanted Peyton to trust him, but he doubted she desired to expose her heart to him again. He wanted to reconnect the bonds he severed and hoped Peyton would accept his pledge to take care of her for the rest of his life. He'd have to wait and see what his future held.

The hours ticked by at a painstakingly slow pace. He'd checked her vital signs, keeping the vigil every thirty minutes. Everything had been normal the past three times. He glanced at the clock then wished he hadn't. Exhaustion finally ruled over him. He disrobed down to his boxers, climbed onto the bed beside Peyton and drew the covers over them. Peyton groaned as if in pain when he cradled her.

"Shh, my bright-shining star. Everything will be okay." Whatever was wrong with Peyton, he'd give his life to save hers.

He brushed her raven hair away from her beautiful face, stroking her high cheekbones with the back of his fingers. Her long eyelashes curling up at the ends lay against her pale skin. Having Peyton nestled against him stirred the memories he had refused to examine until this past year.

The first time they met was at the company Christmas party. He was like any other red-blooded man beckoning her for plain ol' sex. Yeah, he'd hit on her. She laughed and rebuffed his advances until one day she'd given in.

They had dated for well over a year before he asked her to marry him. He'd longed for children, a little girl who looked like Peyton, and a son to throw catch with in the backyard. It wasn't too long afterward, his mother called and spoke to him as though she'd never abandoned her family. His insecurities ignited into an uncontrolled blaze burning every last inch of ground, and the bridge he'd painstakingly built over the years toward trusting women collapsed in the inferno.

Uncertain whether he'd ever heal, he gave in to the firestorm of anxieties. He didn't want to hurt Peyton, but delaying the inevitable would've only caused her more grief so he freed Peyton from the fires of his personal hell. But there was more. Life always had a way of weighing down even the strongest.

Within twelve months, Peyton rose to superstar, writing for the big screen. She'd been willing to take a hiatus from her career to start a family, but the timing wasn't the best for him.

As the firm acquired more criminal cases, his hours increased. He was damn good in contractual law, but he excelled in exonerating alleged desperados, whether guilty or innocent, he didn't care. In fact, he'd done his job so well, when he'd defended numerous icons and won, he became a senior partner. For the first time in the firm's history, names were rearranged.

He and Peyton had leased an apartment on the twelfth floor in the same high rise as his office to alleviate his commute, which meant less down time for him. Every waking hour, he was at his desk. To spend more time with him, she'd bring lunch to the office, and he'd throw it off to the side, pretty much ignoring her presence. One day, she'd asked him, "Are you seeing someone else or is your aversion just directed at me?" He had disregarded her question.

Peyton had made one last effort. She promised him a paradise of beautiful sunsets, walks on the beach, romantic dinners, and plenty of sex. He had chosen not to go to Tahiti. The bottom line, he didn't have a single minute to give to her, and the worst part, the demons from his biological egg donor smothered him until he couldn't breathe. He wished Peyton would have focused on her career, then maybe, and he acknowledge it was a long shot; he would've had time to explain or at least win one battle.

He wanted the white picket fence and all that came with it, but he'd been terrified and a coward for not telling Peyton about his struggles. His fear of Peyton walking away just like his mom had on Easter, Thanksgiving and the last time on Christmas was too much. Back then, his dad actually thought his mother would come back like the other times. When she never returned, Cole detested her and all the holidays, especially Christmas. The recollections were too bitter to forget. Hell, he still refused to forgive the woman who betrayed his family and him. His anxieties had contaminated all his relationships, including the one with Peyton, the very person who had his heart.

Before Peyton left on her vacation, he'd taken the initiative of choosing their favorite restaurant to break off their engagement, figuring they would both leave before ordering. He found her sitting at their table. Peyton grinned when she first saw him, but after she looked closer a frown wrinkled her face. She had sensed something was wrong.

He sat and tried to tell her their relationship was over, but his lips never carried the words he wanted to express.

The emotions skittering across Peyton's eyes ranged from anger to acceptance, then she shut him out completely. She dug into her purse and withdrew the ring. Peyton had known his intent even before she saw him that night. She laid the family heirloom from his father's side on the table in front of him. "Don't bother sticking around. I haven't eaten all day and I'd prefer to dine alone."

He unfolded from his chair.

She pinned him with a beautiful smile. "I'll be out of our—your apartment before my trip. Have a good life."

For someone who had never taken the time or the inclination to reflect on life's journeys, he'd spent the last twelve months trying to figure out how he'd turned into such an asshole or closer to the truth, let his fears rule his heart. How could he treat the one woman he loved with dishonesty? The most important question still remained. How would he correct what he'd messed up three years ago? He had to begin somewhere and trust would be one hell of a start.

He'd planned on finding her, wooing her back into his arms and his life. When Peyton first arrived, he saw her indifference; he'd been hurt and frustrated. As a result, he drove to her cabin and rebuffed her concern. All Peyton had tried to do was to reach out to him. He shook his head once. "Damn." There were times he was a complete idiot.

With Jillian inviting Peyton and the arrival of the blizzard, he may have a chance to win Peyton back. Maybe these were signs of good things to come? Who was he kidding? He believed in facts not coincidences of nature. However, if he could right the wrongs he had committed with Peyton long ago, he'd be one happy man.

Peyton curled her body onto him. Her lips grazed his neck as her tongue flicked across his pulse point. His bright-shining star had given him the happiest times of his life. Back then, he had been too paranoid from his mother's behavior to realize what he had. His hand kneaded Peyton's back, traveling to her flat stomach to play with the silver, belly-button stud.

Peyton's eyelids fluttered open. Golden, desire-laced eyes captured his. Just as quick, her demeanor changed, and she jerked away from him. She cast the blankets off and rolled out of his arms. When she landed on the floor, her feet wobbled then steadied.

His hand shot down to keep the quilt at his waist. No need for her to see how his body reacted to her attentive mouth...just yet.

"What in the hell do you think you're doing in my bed?" Peyton whisked her hair from her face.

"Actually, this is more mine than yours."

She glanced down at her lack of clothing. "Ahh." The shriek erupted from her beautiful rose-hued lips, the ones he wanted wrapped around his shaft. His length hardened into a steel rod as he pictured her nipples the same color as her mouth, which he wanted to taste and savor. From past experience, all he had to do was pay attention to her perky breasts and she would climax.

Peyton grabbed her clothes and tugged them on. She strode out of the room irritated as hell at him.

"That went well." The mattress creaked as he heaved his frame from the bed. He slipped on his jeans and followed the noises coming from the kitchen.

Cole leaned his hip against the counter and crossed his arms against his bare chest, daring her to comment further. While squinting from the white glare of morning sun shining through the cabin windows, three things were on his mind. First, he wanted to find out what had happened to her earlier. Second was to free her of those ridiculous warm-ups shrouding her delicious curves, and third sink into her luscious, wet sheath, preferably all within the next minute. He'd better calm down. Cole gulped at his reflection from the glass cabinet and fingered the purple hue around his right eye. "Care to explain?"

"No." Peyton's hand shook as she set the mug inside the microwave. She closed the door and pushed the number one.

Intrigued by her lack of resolve, he pressed further. "I heard you scream and found you sprawled on the floor where you punched me. I'm sporting a shiner, compliments of you."

The amber metallic flecks glittered under the lighting and her gaze softened. "I didn't mean to hurt you."

"I know." He closed the distance, parting his legs to cradle her groin. When he gathered her in his arms, she angled into his curves. Without prodding from him, her fingers skimmed over his waist and tightened around his back. To let her know the full effect she had on him, his palms pushed her rear to rub against the bulge in his pants.

He floated over the whorl of her ear, expressing in the softest voice he could muster, "You, my love, are killing me."

She placed both hands on his chest and shoved.

"I'm not your anything. Besides, you always woke up with an erection."

"Your premise has too many holes to even begin counting, but I'll give you two. You're assuming you don't mean anything to me and second, that I had fallen asleep last night."

Her hands braced each hip. "Then you and your cock don't care who is in your bed?"

He winced. "Damn, Peyton. When did you get so cynical and a filthy mouth to boot?"

"You loved hearing dirty words… just not mine." She raised her hand. "I'm outta' here."

He grasped her elbow. "Not until you answer my question. You were comatose. Tell me why you think I don't deserve an answer."

"I'm fine. It's nothing for you to be concerned about." She wrenched from his light grip.

Peyton was hiding something, and so far he'd been unable to make any connections. He'd have to change his tactics because she'd never open up with him putting her on the defensive. "I'm worried. Believe it or not, I do care about you."

Worry lines crossed her forehead then she quickly erased them. "Pretending doesn't suit you." She shook her head. "I'm going to take a shower before I go. I'll be out of your hair within the hour."

He strolled to the window and swiped the sheer curtains to each side. "I don't think you're going anywhere soon." Cole released the material. "By the time you get out, I'll have breakfast ready."

Peyton's head tilted to the side and for the first time, her lips curved into a smile. She scampered out of the room. Now that was the woman he remembered.

Cole whistled a lively tune. At first, he had tallied several errors, but he reversed his fouls. Peyton couldn't leave because of the weather and that would give him some time to convince her to try again. The bacon sizzled in the pan as he readied the eggs and bread. He would dazzle her with French toast and his best homemade omelet.

When he nestled Peyton between his legs, she'd responded. After filling her tummy, she'd be putty in his hands, and he would move to phase two of his seduction plan, to let her know she could trust him. He held his breath and released it. He hoped she would give him the benefit of the doubt until he could prove to her he had changed for the better. According to Jill and Leah, he had come a long way.

He lined the cleaned vegetables on the cutting board in a row. All of the knives on this estate were damn sharp, and he'd have to keep his mind on what he was doing. Cole gathered the fresh veggies with his left hand, sliced with his right. Soon, he had a rhythm. The cadence solidified his meandering thoughts back to his work.

Normally, he would've never considered celebrating Christmas with Jill and Richard, let alone visit at this time. Peyton had been his first reason, but the second objective was to make a decision about his job. One of the nagging problems still festered and he had to get away. All of his partners had issued an ultimatum either accept a force buy-out or defend the client. If he chose the former, they had a lot of influence and he'd be black-balled. And he didn't have any jobs lined up, although, he had been thinking of opening his own practice. As for the latter, his gut instinct had never let him down before.

"Shit. That hurt." He wrapped his finger in a paper towel, the blood oozing from his wound spread across the quilted layers. One thing he had going in his favor, he always healed faster than most folks. And if he continued to wield cutlery, he damn well better figure out how to maneuver around his colleagues.

Chapter Three

After her shower, Peyton enthusiastically slathered on the lotion inundated with moisturizers. The dry zephyr air zapped all the natural oils from her skin. Her mouth watered from the aroma drifting into the bedroom. She dressed and bounded for the kitchen to help Cole. Her tummy growled. "Wow, the table is already set and everything smells yummy."

Cole held the chair for her. "Have you taken a gander outside?" After she sat, he settled across from her.

She accepted the meat platter he offered. "Yes, I did. I can't believe it's still snowing, but it's that time of year. If you keep cooking this kind of meal, I'll welcome your company." She winked. "When did you become a chef? Last I remember you couldn't boil water."

"Self-preservation." Cole stabbed several veggies in the omelet. "What have you been up to?" He jammed the food in his mouth.

"The usual. You?"

When Cole swallowed, he smirked. "Another deflection."

"I answered your question, although you haven't acknowledged mine."

"Jilly said you had another screenplay project. Tell me about it." He picked up a slice of bacon with his thumb and forefinger taking a bite.

"Just like you, I can't talk about my job."

"Until it's in the can."

"Then onto my next one. Enough about me. How did *you* get time off?"

"We've never been able to discuss each other's work. Maybe that's why we spent a lot of time in bed."

"Don't go there." She grasped the napkin from her lap and wiped her lips.

"Why not?" His right eyebrow inched higher, and he leaned back in his seat.

"Many reasons." She rose from her chair taking her plate to the sink. "Walking down memory lane isn't a good idea for us."

"Earlier, you responded to me. Admit it, you still want me."

"Did you really think I'd fall for your charms again?" She rinsed off her plate then placed everything into the dishwasher.

Cole grunted. "No…Maybe. Yeah, I guess I did."

"You're an egotistical asshole. If we were the last people on this earth, the human race would end and I wouldn't give a flying fuck."

"I know you're not the same woman I knew three years ago, but I could change your mind." His eyebrows waggled.

"When ducks fly out of my ass."

Cole rose and before his clenched jaw ticked, she saw something in his eyes he hadn't displayed in a long time. "It's not safe for you to leave so I'll clean up and otherwise keep myself occupied…wherever you're not." He wheeled and strode toward the living room.

Her heart ached to see the hurt in his gaze which

transformed into controlled anger. She'd delivered the smart-ass comment out of emotional self-defense. Maybe, it was for the best. Their situation dictated distance between them and she had achieved the goal. Then, why didn't she feel better? And she sure as hell sounded like a bitch. She would squirrel away at the desk in the bedroom and work, keeping as much space between them as she could. Peyton filled her mug with coffee. She meandered to her laptop and set her mind to the script.

The seat creaked every time she shifted her weight and the blasted click of the mantel clock eked out every God-forsaken second. The cursor blinked and the blank page mocked her. "Argh." Peyton whirled around in the chair and hit her knee on the corner of the desk. "Ouch." She rubbed her skin. Cole kept his word, she hadn't seen him. He had consumed her every thought. "Blast the man."

She rose and straightened into a lengthy stretch then edged to the doorway and peeked into the living room. Cole's shoulders spread past the executive leather chair. The folders stacked high on the roll-top desk tipped to one side. When had he carried in his case files? The pen in his hand scratched notes on his legal pad.

Stealthy in her woolen socks, she approached unnoticed, wanting to observe him in action. She loved gazing at his brows furrowed deep in concentration as well as appreciated his cunning expertise in the courtroom.

"I never could tolerate you hovering. Go back to work so I can do mine." His angry bass voice echoed in the great room.

"Feel like taking a break?" She bit her lower lip expecting him to swivel his seat and peg her with a go-to-hell look.

When he turned, his gaze revealed he wanted her in a worse place. A thick exasperated sigh escaped. "If you're relinquishing the master bedroom, I could use a shower."

She notched her chin higher. "You could've taken one in the guest bathroom."

He sprang to his feet. A cross between a growl and a harrumph crossed his lips before he slammed the door.

Peyton plopped in his chair. He'd get over it, she had. She focused on the myriad of files. One in particular caught her eye. Her skin pebbled, and the hair on the back of her neck stood on end. An eerie familiarity inundated her soul. Her hands trembled. She stretched and retrieved the dossier. The tab read Hendricks, James ML

Her thumb and forefinger flipped the heavy cardboard and the image portrayed a stoic picture of Mr. Hendricks. "Oh my God, Pig Man." She scanned through the pages.

She chose the next file on top and perused it hastily examining each leaf of information, then grabbed another. After the eleventh, there wasn't any question in her mind. She methodically returned each to their original position, except one.

"What the hell are you doing?" Cole glowered.

Peyton scrutinized him. Her mouth opened to tell him. She pursed her lips together, rose, pointed, and tried again. Giving up, she closed the legal-size compilation, placed it with the others and retreated to her bedroom. She face planted onto the bed. Her mind wheeled with what she'd found.

The battle of emotions struggled within. Should she tell Cole he was defending a murderer? Could she convince Cole she had witnessed, Hendricks, James ML, the man dressed in black, who had slain every single one of those women—in her mind? Oh and I'd be remiss if I didn't mention the fact, he's slowly killing me too.

"Yeah, right." He would celebrate Christmas before he accepted her word. And she already knew what he thought of that particular holiday. Peyton would rather die first than beg Cole to consider her episodes to be true. Wait, Jillian would vouch for her sanity. Surely, she could persuade Cole using logic.

She snorted. He was a stubborn, mule headed, ass…well, a mule and an ass were not exactly congruent…But if she didn't tell Cole, she'd have innocent blood on her hands.

Within a few minutes, she gathered the strength to face her demons and be at the top of her game to talk to Cole, who was already pissed at her. Peyton entered the living room, angled to the left and secretly studied Cole, perusing his work.

"I've always been able to sense your presence and hear you breathe."

"I never knew that." Her heart skipped a beat. He had shared something of himself.

Cole raised his chin. "I can't discuss these cases with you. And why are you standing behind me? That always drove me nuts. It's like you get a kick out of bothering me."

Her gut clenched and her blood pressure zoomed;

her temple pulsed with each heartbeat. Anger zipped to the depths of her soul. No wonder she could never make their relationship work, he was an ass, not a mule. "With that settled, I have something to say. Your man, Hendricks, is a serial killer."

He grunted.

She retreated to her bedroom, dug out her cell, and tapped the number. "Jillian, I need to leave. When will the foreman have the driveway cleared?"

Peyton panned the room, noting her belongings. "An hour, great. I'm sorry I won't be able to stop and say good-bye." Every time she left, Jill cried, and she didn't have the strength to endure the avalanche of emotions. "Thanks. I love you too. Bye."

She shoved the phone in her back pocket. Sixty minutes later, she strode past Cole with her luggage.

"You're wrong. He had an alibi for every one of the counts against him. What I want to know is how did you identify him? Saw his picture in the paper, on TV or internet news?"

Peyton froze. Tingles shot down her arms to her fingertips and the bags dropped from her grasp. She paused then lowered to the floor and closed her eyes, waiting for the inevitable.

The dark presence slithered over Peyton and covered her like a blanket. The mass penetrated and seeped within, occupying her misty form. An evil miasma wafted to her nostrils and she gasped for a breath.

"Sit in the corner, my sweet thing." James ML Hendricks instructed.

"I'm not—"

"Shut up, bitch." Hendricks' hands wrapped

around her neck and he applied pressure to her windpipe.

She grabbed his wrists and fought. A bracelet gouged her palm, and just as she was ready to pass out, he let go. She coughed and sputtered until she had enough oxygen. If her body was in spirit form, how did he choke her?

"As you can tell, I'm getting stronger. Soon you'll be at death's door." A cackle escaped from Pig Man then changed into maniacal laughter. He was definitely Satan's spawn.

Muffled cries came from across the room. Two young women whimpered. They were possibly in their early twenties, gagged, with their feet and hands bound.

"Why are you doing this?" Peyton shuddered.

"I get more powerful with each one." He smirked.

"Let them go and you can do whatever you want with me. I won't fight."

"What fun is that?" His face lowered within two inches of hers. "I want the terror coursing through their blood and their screams of mercy upon their lips."

The smell of Boudin sausage assailed her senses again. "Oh, God." Without a doubt, this was the same man. Peyton prayed for help, of any kind.

"Time for you to go." He flicked his right wrist.

Peyton's head whirled until she saw double of everything. Her stomach lurched. Struggling to keep awake, she fought the centrifugal force of the maelstrom. Slowly, she succumbed to the blackout.

Chapter Four

Cole shifted in his chair under Jillian's scrutiny.

Jill presented him with the big sister eye while her fingers clutched the coffee cup. "There are times I'm ashamed of you and don't want to claim you as my brother."

Cole toyed with his liquor glass. "Answer one question for me."

Her brows furrowed. "I smell you coming in for a kill. Go ahead, I'll take the bait."

"How in the hell was I supposed to know about her visions?"

Jill lightly touched his forearm. "I'm not condemning you, but you could've handled the situation differently...more delicately."

He threw back the shot of bourbon and swallowed. The burning sensation followed the trail of the amber liquid from his throat to his stomach. "How long does she normally stay unconscious?"

Jillian's concerned gaze changed and he didn't like what he saw, fear and anxiety all wrapped in the depths of her brown eyes. "It depends on the length of time she was in her projected images. Do you remember how long she was...under?"

"I didn't have a stopwatch."

"Stop being a jerk." Jill straightened her spine.

"I'm sorry, hazard of my trade. If I had to guess,

she had been out for well over an hour before you got here. All total, three."

Jillian squinted. "From what Peyton has told me, they are getting longer, but that's an extended period of time. She'll be out for twice that. Be aware, Peyton's blood pressure rises significantly and will have a really bad headache afterward. I've done all I can do for her. I'm worried Cole."

"When did this start, what does she see and why?"

Jillian rose and placed her mug in the dishwasher. "Her experiences are not mine to tell. If you need me, I'll be up at the house. Keep me updated."

Outside, Cole kissed Jilly's cheek. He steadied her until she settled on the ATV. Jill cranked the four-wheeler, gunned the engine and climbed the slippery slope to her house. She crested the incline then dropped from his line of sight.

Once inside the cabin, he closed the door, gathered Peyton's luggage from the living room and stowed her bags in the bedroom closet.

The light from the bathroom filtered in enough for him to see and he wiped her brows from the constant perspiration. He gently removed her outer clothing and smoothed the single sheet over her. In between his fingers, he wove her silken hair through them.

Most of the time, his quick mouth outsmarted and outplayed the majority of people to his advantage, but with Peyton, he'd let his anger override his real wants and desires. His sharp words possibly cut the last thread binding them together. If she hadn't had her episode, she would have been gone, leaving his sorry ass behind. And in this instance, he had been the one to push Peyton away.

When would he learn to be the man she needed? Christ, he'd gladly give up being an attorney if it meant he could have his bright-shining star. Her light filled him with life and he had to admit…love. He figured he had one more chance to make amends with Peyton. Whatever was happening to her, he'd help her overcome it. The problem was he didn't know what the hell was going on. Frustration zapped every nerve ending in his body, his blood pressure rose. He inhaled a calming breath. According to Jilly, Peyton had to tell him. His premonition told him Peyton's troubles stemmed from Hendricks, but that didn't make any sense either. How did Peyton know about the bastard?

The culmination of the data led him to believe the grotesque murders were at the hands of one man. He'd come to a conclusion, Hendricks killed all those women. In a meeting with his partners, he'd voiced those opinions without proof, based purely on gut instinct. Their reaction surprised him. They didn't care if Mr. James ML Hendricks was a serial killer and into voodoo, he was a paying client and specifically requested Cole to defend him. Out of all the lawyers in this country, why did Hendricks choose him?

What he still didn't understand, how did Peyton recognize Hendricks? Hopefully, he could prod her into sharing and come up with some reliable answers. If not, he'd have to pursue other venues which meant he'd alienate himself from the firm. But one thing he was sure of, he wouldn't defend this man who viewed a human life as his playground for butchering. He'd have to call Kevin, the prosecutor for this case.

A moan escaped from Peyton. He cupped her jawline. "My love, come back to me." Literally and figuratively would make him a happy man.

One side of her mouth curved into a half smile. "It appears I never left... My love?"

He slid his palm down her arm, intertwining their fingers. "I'm not going to beat around the bush. I want you back in my life...What do you think about that?"

Her lips thinned to a straight line. "Why?"

"Because we're good together."

Her eyes locked onto his. "Only between the sheets."

He lowered and kissed each fingertip then brushed several on her palm. "I plan to prove you wrong, Peyton Adams. Will you give us a chance?"

Her lips turned into a smile. He jockeyed beside her, gathered her into his arms, and his forehead lightly touched her temple. "Just rest, we'll talk later."

She maneuvered laying half of her body on top of him. Her breathing changed to a relaxed rhythm.

"Sleep well, my love."

He awoke to find her gazing at him. When he splayed his hand on her tummy, her navel dipped and goose bumps rose over her flesh. She physically reacted to his touch. Now, if he could coax her into trusting him. First, he had to set her mind at ease on several issues.

"Are you ready to talk?"

She stiffened.

He stroked from her belly to her hip, down her thigh and back up to catch her hand. Her skin smelled of roses and felt like the soft petals after the flower had just opened. "On several occasions, I didn't treat you very well and I'm sorry." He kept her from moving away. "Just hear me out."

In his arms, she quieted. But her weary eyes scanned his face then fastened onto something over his shoulder. "In the past, I lost sight of what was important to me. I promise not to make that mistake again. Please look at me." He patiently waited for her gaze to latch with his. "Initially, Jillian invited me here. To be honest, I had an ulterior motive to visit. I heard you were staying here for a couple of months. I wanted to see if we could start over. When I saw you, my gut twisted. Then we fought. Instead of talking to you, I reacted like a loser. Forgive me?"

Peyton bit her lower lip between her teeth as he paused holding his breath.

She nodded.

He released the air, ready to tread down the path of step two. "I'd like you to reconsider us, you and me, together."

"You don't share yourself."

"What?"

"I loved watching you work and I never knew you hated it. More specifically and in your words, bothered you. I..." As she shook her head, her hair tickled his arm.

"Again, my battered ego lashed out. I come with flaws, but I'm doing better. Without a doubt, I'm still in love with you."

"No one's perfect. But I can't be involved with anyone. I have some things I need to tell you."

He inhaled deeply through his nose hoping she'd trust him enough to reveal her problems. "Go ahead."

"Since my car accident, I've been having...spells."

She did it. God, Peyton was a strong woman. He urged her on while she was still willing to talk. "Okay."

"Because of those episodes, I'm not...can't allow you and me...to become an us."

"What?" He shook his head. "Why?"

She released him, rolled off the bed and paced the length of the room. "Come on, even you should be able to foresee the difficulties. I have about a fifteen second warning. I drive state highways so I can pull over. When I have speaking engagements, I hire an assistant. I can't have children under my watch." Her fingers indicated each reason.

Water welled in her eyes. "With each one, my recoveries are taking longer. Eventually, I'll never wake up...All I'll ever be to you or anyone is a burden. I can't put you through this horrific situation I'm going through. So...you see, I must walk away...You deserve better." She ran into the bathroom and slammed the door closed.

If Peyton thought he couldn't get in, she was in for a surprise. He bounced from the bed, strode to what Peyton believed was a barrier between them and pounded twice on the wood frame. "Don't push me away. I'll hire a nanny and a driver."

Chapter Five

Peyton's heart ached at the thought of shutting Cole out of her life, but she had to. If he kept asking her, she wouldn't have the strength to continue to refuse him. How could he be so blind? In the end, he'd find someone to love. She had to be the strong one for both of them.

The pain surfaced from deep within her broken soul. Life was unfair and Hendricks had the upper hand. Drying the wet streaks from her cheeks, she straightened her spine resolving to put Pig Man behind bars while she still had more waking hours than unconscious ones. Truthfully, she didn't know how long she had. When she opened the door, Cole towered over her. His hands grasped each side of the threshold.

"I want to put the man you're defending in jail. Will you be with me or against me? She swallowed hard waiting for his answer.

His gaze fixed onto hers. "Believe it or not, I think he's guilty too. How did you know...your visions?"

"You're fast." She ducked under his arm and marched toward Cole's desk.

Several hours later, Cole closed the last file. "How strange your episodes began when you were in Louisiana. The car accident happened on your way there, so I'm not sure you can blame the wreck."

"I viewed the collision as though it jostled my

brain. Kind of like radio signals via new fillings syndrome."

Cole laughed. When he settled, he swiped his fingers through his hair. "I'm wondering if there may be a possibility of intervention."

"What are you talking about? I'm not an alcoholic or on drugs." Peyton paled at Cole's thought process. Was the next step placing her in an institution?

"You jumped to the wrong conclusion." Cole shook his head once. "I'm speaking of black magic."

"That's nonsense. You don't believe in that stuff and I only write about it." She rose and strolled to the window. For whatever reason, the outdoors always soothed her frayed nerves. A bird on a snow covered branch captured her attention then the feathered creature flew away.

"Jilly had said Leah was researching something down there. Maybe, I can phone her and get her to check on a few things for me." Cole withdrew his cell and initiated the call.

Peyton needed fresh air. She stepped outside and exhaled; seeing her breath, she crossed her arms to ward off the chill. The cold crept over her frame inundating her with a stern warning. An alarm bell rang inside her mind as she remembered the toxic memories of each crime scene. Every time Hendricks confronted her with his victims, the atmosphere was hot and muggy. How odd she never realized the temperature of the surroundings, until now.

The door opened and Cole joined her. His chest snuggled against her back. "You're shivering."

"I swear I wasn't two seconds ago." Her teeth shattered and her body shook.

"I didn't mean to scare you about the voodoo stuff." Cole rubbed his hands up and down her arms.

"Wha-what di-did Le-ah have to sa-say?"

"You should come inside. I can't have my bright-shining star catching the flu."

Her knees buckled. Cole caught her before she hit the ground. "Peyton?"

"Y-you sou-sound stra-strange." Cole's voice seemed as though he were a thousand miles away talking through a megaphone. Her head swam, and her vision blurred. She succumbed to the vortex.

When she opened her eyes, a pile of blankets had been draped over her. Cole must have been trying to keep her warm. She had stopped shivering, the heaviness of the covers felt good, just like when Cole made love to her. His weight had always given her a sense of security she never understood. Even though she acknowledged they couldn't have a relationship, deep down she truly missed Cole's touch, his kisses, and above all, their joining. "What happened?"

Cole sat on the edge of the couch. She scooted over to give him more room. His forehead wrinkled with concerned lines and he grasped her chin until her gaze connected with his. "You passed out."

"This one wasn't like the others." Moisture clouded her vision. What was Satan's spawn doing to her?

"Tell me what happened out there." Cole's fingers brushed her hair to the side.

"You're going to think I'm crazy."

"No, I won't."

She might as well tell Cole everything, maybe then he would realize they could never be a couple. "When

Hendricks makes me watch him torture his victims, I have a warning and the environment is hot and humid. Afterward, there is a curtain of darkness that shrouds my consciousness and I feel like I'm falling into a maelstrom. Eventually, I wake up with a migraine and very weak. With each occurrence, he forces me to stay longer in his hell.

"Go on." Cole's ice-blue eyes watered.

"This past time, I was sucked in a whirlwind with debris, like a tornado. I was freezing, couldn't catch my breath and knew I was going to fall to my death. But something or someone stopped me before I hit the ground."

"God, I feel…so helpless." He thumbed tears from his eyes. "But we'll figure this out, okay?"

She swiped the moisture he'd missed and was surprised Cole let his emotions show. "Are you really going to stick with me on this or are you going to run for California as fast as you can?"

"If you never trust me in anything else, believe this. I won't leave you."

She nodded. Cole had never spoken in terms of a couple even when they were. On numerous occasions, he had shooed her away and told her he would text what they would do. Not once did Cole ask for her input. Under no circumstances were they a team. However, that was the past. Now, Cole had changed for the better. She would have to be blind not to see his transformation. She relaxed knowing he had her back and that he possessed the wherewithal to handle this situation. She sure didn't.

"I'll be with you every step of the way. If there is anything else you remember that could help me piece this together, I want to know immediately. Meanwhile, I need to try Leah again and Sparks never returned my call."

Peyton tilted her head.

"Kevin Sparks is a colleague, a friend and the prosecutor for this case. Also, I want Leah to check on a few things while she's in New Orleans."

"While you do that, I'll go fix us some lunch." She withdrew her hands from underneath the pile of blankets.

Lunch? "No, you need to rest. I'll pull together an early dinner." *And find out what the hell is going on.*

Chapter Six

In the kitchen, Cole tapped through the menu until he found Leah's number and hit connect. "Hey sis, how are you?"

"Fine, how 'bout you, Linc?" Leah's pet name drove him crazy and he'd pay her back in kind.

"You know I'm always good, Snake."

"Forgot about that one. You never call me, so who died?"

"No one. Have a question."

"Shoot."

"I need you to interview and hire a team of private investigators and send all the bills to me. Here's the clincher, they need to believe in black magic or at least a possibility there is some truth to the matter."

"Where are you?" His sister's demeanor changed.

"At Jilly's and something is happening to Peyton. And it's not good."

"I know."

"How?"

"Another topic for a different day." Leah's exhausted tone created a coil of worry that tightened around his head and radiated down his body.

"You don't sound good. I can have someone else—"

"NO." Leah cleared her throat and whispered, "I need to do this."

"What aren't you telling me?" He should've video conferenced this call to observe Leah's physical reactions as opposed to identifying and understanding her masked inflections which she was damn good at hiding.

"Just watch over Peyton."

The background noise changed to a cruel silence. With Leah in New Orleans and Peyton here, how could he safeguard his loved ones? He rubbed the back of his neck with his hand and massaged the taut muscles.

"You bet I will. Sis, be careful."

"Always."

He fingered end, phoned Kevin, asked him to check on a few things and called in a favor. Kevin would have Leah followed for protection. Maybe he'd have some answers after Christmas and Leah would be okay, for now.

He strode to the living room. While he repositioned the blankets, Peyton slept soundly. He kissed her forehead and went to the kitchen and began supper.

****

"Hey you're up. How ya' feeling?" Cole cautiously studied Peyton.

"Much better. Let me help." Peyton's color was back and she smiled.

"Sounds like a plan." Seeing his bright-shining star stronger and happier, he whistled a jovial Christmas song. Imagine that. His contentment came from Peyton and she seemed to be the one healing him.

After they ate, both of them cleaned the kitchen. Peyton turned from the sink. "Cole?"

"Yeah?" He hung the tea towel over the top handle of the double oven.

"I need a hug."

He clasped Peyton's arms bringing her within his embrace and gently squeezed. When he released his hold, her hooded eyes shouted desire. He lowered kissing her soft lips. She opened and he delved his tongue into her mouth. The sweet flavor of a power drink burst across his taste buds. He angled for deeper access and she granted it to him.

Her hips undulated. His hard-on strained the boundaries of his denims. He grasped each side of her shoulders and eased her back several inches. What he saw he'd gladly give to her. "Are you sure?"

When she nodded, he gripped the hem of her sweatshirt along with her camisole and whisked the clothing over her head, letting them drop to the floor. All the while, she'd been divesting her pants and started on his. Now, both lay in a pool at their feet.

He wanted to make this joining special for his bright-shining star, give her joy and if he couldn't sway her to stay with him, he'd always have something to remember her by. His hands curved around her rear, lifting her until her pelvic bone met his groin. She wrapped her legs around his waist, locking her ankles. As he walked to the dining table, her essence flowed over him and he moaned. "You're ready for me."

He snatched several thick towels from a drawer. "Use these. On your knees baby, with your back to me." Once positioned, he gently lowered her shoulders. With her sassy ass in the air, he palmed the fleshy globes. Her satin skin was smooth and she called his name. His finger followed the crevice finding her slick folds. Her juices flowed over the three fingers he had inserted. He licked his lips wanting to taste her, but he would wait.

He withdrew then separated the cheeks of her butt, sliding his forefinger through the tight ring. She mewled and relaxed. He added another, gliding to the next knuckle. With his other hand, angling from the front side, he slipped into her wet core, he added pressure to her bud with his palm. The thin skin between the channels allowed him to feel his movement along with her muscle responses. She shifted her hips in the air. He sensed she wanted more sensations. He released his left hand and guided his shaft through the slick folds, swirling the honeyed nectar over him. She answered him with a purr and he couldn't wait any longer.

In one movement, he seated his entire length in her. Her warm folds clamped down. "Cole."

****

Peyton's skin pebbled under Cole's touch. This was what she wanted. His undivided attention and the pure bliss of the one place Cole took her. She would never let him stay with her. This was the last time they'd be together so she accepted the ecstasy only he could give her.

Cole's hoarse voice echoed in her ear while his fingertips found her nub. She slid one hand to cup his balls while the other twisted her nipple. Her pulse hammered, her blood pumped, and her hair clung to her sweat-ridden temples. She voraciously milked him, loving his hard-on reaching the remote depths of her core, the lonely depths of her interior that she had kept in isolation, until now.

Cole lightly slapped the bundle of nerves, electricity shot through her system, responding to the pleasure he gave her. He remembered. Automatically, her hands released him. Her knees widened, slanting her hips toward him for more.

He chuckled. "Hmm, you still like it." He popped her again.

Between hearing his erotic inflection, the sensation of his metered thrusts, her apex neared. "Harder."

"Whatever you want."

Cole grasped her hips and plunged. His retreats and advances stoked her passion. The sound of skin cracking through the air fed her like an aphrodisiac. "I'm so close."

His hand snaked around to the bundle of nerves. "Here's your launch baby." He tweaked the swollen nub then swatted.

Her body tensed then released. Blinded by sheer rapture, her orgasm projected her into the skies of a heavenly snowstorm. She floated down like the icy crystals outside, landing softly in his embrace.

Cole's chest met her back, one arm wrapped across her breasts, the other her waist. "I thought you were going to collapse."

Drugged by the love potion only he could give to her, she shook her head.

The next thing she knew, his fingers and thumbs tweaked both of her nipples at the same time, pulling them taut, releasing, and repeating. One hand traveled to her folds, opening her, he caressed the tiny pearl.

Surprised by her already ardent need, she moaned, "Please."

Cole whispered near her ear. "What do you want, my bright-shining star?"

"Don't stop."

"This is just the start, sweetheart."

He withdrew. "As much as I like this position, I want to watch you come." Lifting her off the table, her feet found the floor, but her knees buckled under her weight. Luckily, he kept her from falling.

"Enough of this." He gathered her legs with his forearm and the other cradled her back, he easily picked her up and carried her to the bedroom.

He placed her on the edge of the high country bed, stacking pillows under her rear until her back and shoulders flattened against the mattress.

The passion in his gaze encouraged her to be more brazen. She spread her knees apart.

"How beautiful." Cole's pupils dilated revealing his need. He grasped the base of his shaft and stroked. There was nothing more erotic than to watch Cole pleasure himself.

He closed the distance between them and with the tip, he massaged her nub, applying just the right amount of pressure as he slid between her folds. Her juices coated his engorged shaft, her nerve endings kicked into high gear. A paradise she'd never forget.

She gazed at Cole as his hips thrust then retreated. His sinewy abdomen flexed with every advance and withdrawal. She shivered in anticipation of what was next. Cole's eyes were closed and his jaw locked as though exercising restraint with every movement. He never lost control, even when he was angry.

He opened his eyes. The fire raging from them consumed her like dry kindling. She massaged her breasts while her fingers clenched the hardened tips. "Cole."

"Hmm." The strangled sound seemed incongruous

to the virile man who stood before her.

"Inside me."

"I'm pleasuring you." A rumble deep from his lungs escaped.

"Please."

A second later, the angle of his thrust raked across her sweet-spot and she gasped.

He groaned, which filled her with satisfaction. The muscles she used to excite him awarded her just as much enjoyment. She clamped hard. Intense hunger dominated his expression.

Cole raised one eyebrow while the ends of his lips curled in a grin. With his fingertips, he opened her folds, curving his palm, he gently slapped her bundle of nerves. Her hands freed her breasts. She snaked them above her head and clasped the covers. She wouldn't relinquish her gaze either. "Again."

The stimulating jolt of arousal led her to the threshold once more. This time she offered him everything she had, she grasped and squeezed his shaft. In return, his hips gyrated with power and pumped. Cole incited her to the peak of pure rapture and inside, he rasped all of her pleasure points.

He changed position. Guiding her legs up in the air, leaning them close together against his chest, her feet pointing toward the ceiling, then he slowly entered. His hands journeyed to her hips and his metered movements increased.

The sensation of him leaving a wet path between her feminine lips and thighs, her breasts joining the motion of his movement, titillated her to the brink of madness. "I'm going to climax."

"Baby, I can tell. Keep your eyes open." He

hammered harder and faster. "Go, I want to feel your spasms around me when you come."

She released a scream. Cole held onto her gaze. Tears welled in her eyes and he'd become a fuzzy outline. When she landed, she focused on Cole not moving a muscle.

"So sweet, baby." He withdrew to the tip of his velvet hard-on. At an agonizingly slow pace, he entered her core.

Once fully seated, he growled, "I. Can't. Hold. Back." His muscles tightened. With one last thrust, he arched his back. "Oh, baby." He ground out through clenched teeth.

With her inner muscles, she squeezed him feeling his warm essence fill her.

His eyelids closed then opened. His hands glided from her hips up to her knees. Gently, he withdrew, holding her legs, he slowly lowered them, and placed her feet on the floor. Scooping up the wash cloth he'd used earlier, he solicitously wiped her clean then himself. He tossed the pillows at the headboard. As he rolled onto the mattress, he brought her with him. A heavy sigh discharged from his lungs, cradling her in his arms.

This was one of her favorite times, cuddled against Cole's frame after post-coital bliss. Damn, she missed the many things they did together, too many to count, but there were also too many tears shed to think about. When they broke up, she had expended an enormous amount of energy crying, missing Cole's humor and finally accepting the inevitable.

She draped one leg over his hips and squeezed, letting him know, she appreciated his attention. He had said things would be different, but she knew this was just sex. *It had to be.*

Within minutes, their steady breaths were in unison. Gradually, she cooled down and drifted to sleep.

Peyton awoke and blinked. Cole lay on top of her, his teeth nipping her breast and his hips nestled between her thighs, they had both loved morning sex. Her palms curled around his head, her fingers slid through his thick hair, keeping his tender affection there. Her back arched for more and he delivered, suckling while his tongue flicked over the hardened tip.

Spreading her thighs further, Cole opened her folds and directed his thick tumescent shaft into her core. Her breath hitched as he seated himself completely. The feeling of warmth, fullness and an emotion she wanted to hold on to consumed her.

Where did that thought come from? With her horrifying visions, she could never give any man her entangled life. What in the hell was she thinking? All she wanted was to take what Cole was willing to give…right? No entanglements, no relationship.

When he withdrew, she had the sensation of abandonment. Her first reaction was to follow, but he returned. He chuckled. "Patience." His husky voice bathed her in promise.

He plunged forward. Her hands followed the linear line of his spine and cupped his tightened buttocks. The motion shifted, increasing in speed, accelerating into an intense rhythm until her fevered core begged for more.

The sound of them joining harmonized to their thrusts. Cole rested his weight on one elbow while his hand snaked down and rubbed the pearl between her folds. "You ready? Keep your eyes open."

When she nodded, he tweaked the bundle of nerves between his finger and thumb. She launched like a rocket heading to the starry Milky Way galaxy. The next cognizant moment, Cole's lopsided grin held her focus. The darkened desire in his eyes shot shivers scurrying across her heated skin. Still seated inside her, his shaft jerked. A delicious throb generated once more, and she hungered for his climax.

His mirth vibrated from his chest and tickled her breasts. With every word, he plunged and retreated. "You're perfect in every way, ready for one more?" He stilled and kissed her forehead. "Then I'm going to treat you to one of my special omelets."

"Sounds wonderful. The omelet too."

He pulled out and in a single bound, his feet hit the floor. "Come here, baby."

She scooted across the bed. His hands at each side of her hips, he flipped her and placed her feet to meet his on the throw rug. Her belly flat on the bed, he widened her legs. She heard rustling behind her, then the crinkle of foil, latex snapping and a squirt.

Both lubed palms spread her butt cheeks. He fingered the dark channel readying her for him. She breathed deep, relaxing the tight ring.

"That's it, baby, let me in."

His finger slipped out, then the crown slid past the tight circle. Inching down the chamber, the pain changed to pleasure as he seated himself fully. Cole's gentle rhythm accelerated a craving for more. As if he sensed she needed her appetite sated, his cadence changed to a faster pace. His sacs pelted against her bared folds, she cupped his fleshy treasure in her hand desiring them to slap her tiny bundle of nerves until her climax.

Cole eased back and forth ever so slow. He purposely took his sweet time.

"Faster."

Beads of moisture dropped on her spine and gathered in the indentation. "Cole, please."

He drove in then out. More sweat trickled down her back. The dynamic of his penetration was delectable, the friction titillated her clit. She wanted more stimulation. "Harder."

Cole plunged.

Fire burned from her belly to the depths of her core. The room spun with each advance and withdrawal. Her climax approached as he sank deeper eliciting a fiery blaze from within.

He swatted her rear and carnal satisfaction shot through her entire body. The vibration of his balls slapping her folds, his groin pelting her rear and his groans of gratification echoed in the room. "Cole."

"Go baby, I'm right behind you."

That was a pun if she ever heard one. Was it seconds later or minutes, she couldn't tell. When she came down from the ecstasy of her climax, he shuddered with his release. His semi-rigid shaft twitched inside her. Without losing their connection, his knees found the bed, and lay on top of her. Cocooned between the bed and Cole's chest, the weight taken by his forearms, she reveled in the heat emanating from him. His breaths tickled her neck. She would treasure these memories forever in her isolated future.

Chapter Seven

"I think this will be a good time to get to know one another again." Cole swigged from his coffee cup, and when he swallowed, his Adam's apple bobbed.

"What?" Peyton slid the last bite of her eggs to the side of plate with her fork.

"You heard me."

"I think...we already started don't you?" She laughed. He was acting strange this morning. The emotional entanglements were normally hers to bear.

"That's not what I meant, Peyton and you know it."

"Don't add anything extra to what happen."

His right eyebrow inched higher and he leaned back in his seat. "What are you saying?"

"Sympathy sex. That's all that was."

"Well, now that I know what one feels like, I'll just mosey onward." He rose. His clenched jaw ticked on the right side. He wheeled and strode to the living room

Seated in front of her desk, the echo of her intimate releases with Cole rang in her ears. Peyton tried to forget how he consumed her every thought. The bed ridiculed her. Again, the blank page was a constant reminder that she hadn't succeeded to wipe Cole from her mind. She had said some pretty mean things. Sympathy sex, what in the world was she thinking? He had been attentive and loving. She should apologize for her behavior. Peyton rose from her chair and found

Cole diligently working at the roll top desk.

"Feel like taking a break?" She waited for the same response he gave before.

An exasperated sigh escaped from Cole.

He had taken her smart ass comment to heart. "I'm sorry for what I said earlier. I was out of line."

"Want to go snow-shoeing?" Cole swiveled to face her.

****

Cole grinned as Peyton squealed.

"Yes, lets." She jumped up and down and clapped while her pony tail bounced.

"Get ready and I'll meet you outside."

Cole waited for Peyton to close the front door. "Come and sit on the steps, I'll help you."

She gingerly sat and gave him her right foot. Several minutes later, he had both feet harnessed. He offered his hand. "Up." Then he gave her two poles.

"Where we headed?" Peyton jabbed both of them into the snow.

"The lake."

"How far is it?"

"About a half a mile and well worth every step."

He had always enjoyed sharing outdoor activities with Peyton. She took great care of her body, mind and spirit. He figured this was a perfect opportunity to share and get to know one another again, beyond the bedroom. And in their case, he had to include the kitchen table. Maybe once she relaxed, Peyton would let their relationship happen naturally instead of fighting him. Little worry lines spider-webbed at the corner of her eyes that weren't there before. Yes, he had noticed, but he thought they were from stress of her job, certainly not anxiety.

"There's a path through the woods we can take. Follow me." He set an easy pace and she trailed behind. Once he forged a footpath in the virgin snow, it would be easier for Peyton.

She kept up without complaint and zero conversation, which was not the old Peyton he knew. When they were dating then engaged, she would talk until the next blue moon occurred. Maybe, he didn't know her as well as he gave himself credit for. And what was with the sympathy sex? That blew his ego to hell and back.

A plan, he needed an outline, a strategy by the time they got to the lake. He drew a deep cleansing breath into his lungs. With Peyton, he'd have to use more than his smile as a tactic. She'd require a heavy dose of...He blew the air out...Like he actually knew what women wanted. Well, he used to. A good dinner at an expensive restaurant, high-priced wine and most of them just wanted a roll in the sack. Which he obliged and had fun. But that was years ago, before he admitted that he still loved Peyton. He had to show her how much he cared and changed.

"Oh wow." Peyton smiled as she stepped from the tree line to the beach of the shore. "It's beautiful."

"Richard had a good idea when he built this." He led the way to the park bench nestled under the boughs of several evergreens. His arm swiped the crusted snow to the ground and revealed the wooden slats. Peyton helped brush the icy crystals off the tarp and yanked the canvass from the pit. Wood lay ready in the hearth to light.

Cole opened his backpack, withdrew the dried

kindling and tossed the tinder underneath the stack then used the propane lighter from the cabin and lit the tiny sticks. Once the fire ignited, he added several more logs piled beside the pit.

"Regular boy scout aren't you?"

"Make that Eagle."

"I didn't remember. I'm impressed. My turn." She whisked the straps of her pack from her shoulders and let the bench hold its contents. She dug out water, peanut butter crackers and trail mix.

"Glad we are only going to be gone for a couple of hours."

"Oh, shush." She withdrew the sandwiches she must have made earlier and jerky. "And for dessert." A bag of marshmallows followed the chocolate bars and graham crackers. "Yummy."

"I know what my next job is, whittling."

"Perceptive. But I have that covered, too." Two wire hangers emerged.

"Anything else in that satchel?"

"How did you know?" She produced a flask.

"What's in it?"

Peyton twisted the cap off of the leather pouch and squeezed. "Hmm, wonderful."

She handed him the container and he inhaled. "Peach schnapps. Baby, now we're living the high life."

Peyton laughed out loud. He hadn't heard that beautiful sound in ages.

"Sit and I'll help you out of the shoes."

He knelt before her, wrestled them off and lingered. Her gaze met his and a new calm settled in his gut, somehow he would make Peyton his.

She tilted her head to the side. "What are you

thinking?"

"How beautiful you are." He cleared his throat, rose and put all the food stuff back in her bag then settled beside her. "Jill and Richard offered to sell me some acres, right over there." He pointed across the lake. "For a very reasonable sum I might add, to build a house. I'm thinking I should."

"That's great." Peyton fidgeted and scooted to the edge, away from him.

"I can visualize raising two kids here. Teaching them to swim and fish."

"That's nice. Dating anyone special to share your future?" She rose, sidled over to the pit watching the flames. The only sound was the constant crackle from the blaze.

"I have my eyes on someone." He joined her and slid his arm around her shoulders.

Peyton flinched and shoved him forcing his forearm to drop to his side. "Congratulations, I hope everything works out for you." She strode to the shoreline.

Cole trailed her footsteps and stopped behind her. He placed his palms on her hips, tugged Peyton's back against his chest then embraced her.

"Don't. I can't believe you want to marry someone and we were together. You haven't changed at all. Still the same stud." She tried to pull away from him, but he refused to let go.

"Baby, the woman I have in mind is you."

"What we have is temporary." Her chin lowered.

He bristled. "Why?"

"I can't make any plans for a future."

"I see." What she failed to say was with him. He

released her. The calm he had experienced moments ago was gone and anger rose from the fiery depths of his soul, because he had screwed up three years ago.

When she turned to face him, tears glistened in her eyes. "Do you? Did anything I told you earlier sink in or are you still playing hero? I'm not going to saddle you with my problems."

"Can't or won't."

"Does it matter?"

"There's a big difference."

She whirled and trotted to her backpack, withdrew the liquor and guzzled. "Ahh, much better."

He shadowed each of her steps and stood beside her. Peyton slammed the flask to his chest. "Here, drink."

"Yes, ma'am." He squeezed the pouch shooting the fruity mixture into his mouth, and swallowed. "Let's sit and soak up the fire's warmth."

"Love to…This could easily become my favorite place." Peyton sat near the end of the bench and placed her backpack between them.

Yep, he had a long ways to go. He'd ply her with the warming brew. If he remembered correctly, she talked incessantly under the influence and he looked forward to hearing her zany stories.

Chapter Eight

Peyton finished the last sentence and typed 'The End'. After New Year's, Cole had returned to California. That was a month and a half ago. He'd called several times, using the speaker. Cole kept their conversations professional surrounded by Kevin, paralegals, and staff. He and his partners had strategically used this case in a marketing campaign to further themselves in the public eye. 'We do the right thing' was their tag line. Hendricks' bail had been revoked, and he'd been in jail for several weeks.

She was delighted for Cole and satisfied he filled his life with what he loved, work. Funny, she was happy too. Peaceful would be a better term, no heartache, tears and certainly no regrets. She was getting stronger every day, even gained some weight.

Every day until Cole left, they had visited their special spot by the lake, and she continued to seek the solace her favorite place provided. She loved Cole with all of her heart, and acknowledged she would take whatever he was willing to give her.

Her visions had stopped before Cole left. Confident she could drive without having any spells, she had her bags packed and would leave at daybreak. Earlier this evening, after dinner, she had said her goodbyes to Richard and Jillian. She promised them both she'd keep in touch.

The early morning sun shone and Peyton slipped on her sunglasses enjoying the beauty of Montana's countryside. The monochrome palate of the landscape captured her eye. She inhaled the fresh air and exhaled. This was what life was all about. She climbed into her car, started the engine and headed for home. For the first time in over a year, she traveled the interstate. The highways were cleared and she looked forward to sleeping in her own bed tonight.

By late afternoon, a swirl of nausea hit her stomach. She should've stopped for something to eat, but opted to put more hours on the road. Afraid she was going to hurl, she wrapped an arm around her belly and waited for the next exit. Finally, a ramp appeared. She took it, pulled over to the shoulder, and shut the ignition off. What should have been tingles were now stings. Each prick felt like venom had been deposited below her skin. Her flesh hurt.

"Oh, God." The throbs of pain radiated to every part of her body and sweat trickled down her temples, back, and in between her breasts, pooling inside her bra.

"No, you can't do this anymore," she screamed as the maelstrom sucked her in.

"Welcome. Glad you joined me." Hendricks' evil eyes squinted.

"How did you get out?" Peyton swiped her hair to the side.

"I have more power than you ever thought about. Now is the time, dear one. I'm done playing games."

****

Cole burst through the double doors, panning the ICU waiting room. When he saw Jillian and Richard, he released a sigh of relief they were here for Peyton and to receive any updates from the doctors. Jill sprang from the chair, running to him. He opened his arms adjusting his feet for a better stance and caught her inertia.

Tears ran unchecked down her cheeks and she hiccupped between each word. "They're going through a battery of tests."

His chin rested on top of her head. "And." Chills inundated his soul as he waited for the answer.

"That's all I know."

Richard's nod said hello while he gently grasped his wife's shoulders and lingered until Jilly released him.

With Richard's help, he guided Jillian to her seat. The digital wall clock illuminated the minutes turning into hours.

The hydraulic door opened, a gentleman in blue scrubs emerged. "I'm told friends of Peyton Adams are waiting?"

All three of them were ushered into a family counseling room. The doctor's brow lowered, dark circles under his eyes gave away the number of hours he'd been working. "Ms. Adams has been in a state of unconsciousness since she arrived. She has no apparent injuries, but her organs are shutting down. I can't find a reason for this anomaly. There's another problem. According to the physician's directive found in her purse dated several months ago, I'm only allowed to give her comfort."

"I'll have an injunction by tomorrow morning." Cole turned and grasped the door handle.

"Do you really want to go against Peyton's wishes? Besides that issue, her body is literally quitting. I ran a multitude of tests and there are no medical explanations. Therefore, I'm making her comfortable as I can."

Cole released the knob and faced the doctor. "Can I see her?"

"Normally, only relatives are allowed, but from what I understand she doesn't have any."

"Yes, she does. We're her family." Jillian's voice emitted strength contrary to how she was several hours ago.

Inside Peyton's room an EKG beeped her slow heartbeats. Cole waited in the corner as he watched Jill and Richard give encouragement. Furiously, he blinked to rid the moisture in his eyes. When they left to give him privacy, he made his way to the side of the bed.

Cole slid his hand in Peyton's. Cold fingers met his and the bluish color of her fingernails indicated the lack of blood flow. Even her skin had a grayish tint.

He kicked off his shoes and crawled in beside her, gathering her into his arms. "Peyton, don't give up." He kissed her temple then journeyed down to her jawline and across where he lightly pressed on her unresponsive mouth.

Not one to admit defeat, he nestled her into his folds and rested her head in the crook of his neck. Silent sobs racked his chest while his tears gathered finally dripping down his cheeks.

Nurses came and went with each shift change. On the third day, Peyton licked her lips. He grabbed a wet cloth and squeezed, water drops dribbled into her mouth. "Come back to me my bright-shining star."

"Cole?" He barely heard her words.

"I'm here."

"Take me to our cabin."

"Allow the doctor to give you liquids. Your visions stopped while Hendricks was in jail, but he was released due to a paperwork error. That's why all this is happening. I swear we'll find him again, figure out how he has control over you and why in the hell he's doing this to you. Give yourself...and me a chance...please."

"Different." He leaned closer. "I'm not going to make this."

"I want you to fight. Hendricks' is pissing with you, but you'll have to be strong until we can catch him."

"I'm scared."

"Me too." He mouthed silently.

"I'm going to ring the nurse and you have to ask for help."

"Just enough to get me to the cabin."

At this moment, he'd take whatever he could get from Peyton.

Chapter Nine

Cole closed the cabin door as the home health nurse left.

He'd called Richard first to arrange Peyton's move and Kevin second. He yelled at everyone from the detective agency he and Leah had hired, to the police, and his poor secretary caught his wrath also, all to no avail. With still no one able to pinpoint Hendricks whereabouts, he watched Peyton's condition deteriorate.

Peyton vacillated between bouts of freezing to all out sweating. Right now, the blankets piled high kept her warm and he added his own body heat ninety percent of the time. He knew what that meant, Hendricks had captured her mentally. The other ten, Cole would throw the covers off of Peyton and wash her face from the constant perspiration. Damn Hendricks, he had added more victims to his growing list. He contacted Kevin and the authorities to warn them.

He fought the only way he knew how, through the legal system, but judicial procedures had always been a slow process and this time was no different. He didn't know how much longer Peyton had. His stomach tightened and he wanted to punch someone, preferably Hendricks. Cole would kill the bastard if he ever saw him.

"Cole?"

"Yeah?"

"Can you carry me to the lake?"

"No! It's freezing outside." Had she lost her ever loving mind?

"Please?"

"Jesus Peyton, you're asking too much from me. I don't want you to die. Every time I ask you to accept help, you refuse." His chin lowered to his chest, tears filled his eyes at the injustice of it all.

Helpless, that's what he felt. He wanted to give her everything, but the cost was too steep. It meant she'd depart from his world. The only love of his entire existence kept asking him to stand here and watch her die. He wasn't a praying man, but he prayed for Peyton, hoped for strength, and begged that he could make a difference.

"You're right…I shouldn't have burdened you…very selfish." He scarcely heard the whispered words.

If he granted her last wish and took her to their special place, she wouldn't make it. Peyton would perish in his arms. Did he have the right to deny her final request?

In his mind, he rendered the decision automatically. He wielded the clear mind and the power to keep her safe. The caretaker must have the backbone to determine right from wrong and what was best for the loved one.

But at the end of Peyton's life, was he entitled to supersede her appeal? Unequivocally, the resounding answer would be yes, again. He stood beside the bed, mesmerized by Peyton's beauty even when she was at deaths door.

His conscious battled the pros and cons. His gut knotted and his heart ached. He acknowledged, he wouldn't deny her last request. Wrapping Peyton in the blankets, he raised her small frame to his chest and carried her on their final journey together.

The bitter wind blew as he sat down on the bench under the trees. He shivered and cradled her in his arms protecting her from the chilled air. "We're here, baby. I love you." He didn't think he could cry anymore, but he was wrong.

The late afternoon drew to a close and the setting sun meant another day had passed without finding Hendricks or relief for Peyton.

He lit the fire pit, reminisced out loud about his childhood, humorous anecdotes and his silly sisters. Under the guise of protecting them, he had followed Jillian and Leah on their dates in high school. Yeah, he was a pain in their backside.

"We even gave each other nicknames. Jill was named Cinderella because her chore was to clean out the fireplaces. Leah's was snake since she hated them and mine was Link. When I was a teenager, I looked like a string bean, tall and lanky."

Peyton never commented or stirred. The full moon rose and as it began to set, he asked for her forgiveness. He buried his face in her hair and howled like an animal.

Once he calmed, his swollen eyes and blurry vision added to the loneliness and desolation. He shut them, choosing not to witness what he understood was inevitable, life without Peyton by his side.

He awakened and blinked, the morning had almost

broken. Richard gripped his shoulder and shook him. "Hey. I want you to meet some people. They're at the cabin. Give Peyton to me, I'll carry her."

Groggy with what he figured was only an hour sleep, he bent over. Cole hovered above Peyton's mouth. Her breath tickled his skin. She was still alive. He nodded to Richard.

When Cole entered the cabin, his flesh tingled from the heat. The couch and tables were pushed back with men and women gathered in a circle.

An old woman wearing pants and a floor length tunic approached. Her long gray hair surrounded her wrinkled face. She giggled at him then became serious. "My name is Vadoma." She pointed to the center. "Put her inside our ring."

Richard lowered Peyton, laying her on the Persian rug. Vadoma murmured something to his brother-in-law and Richard glanced at him. "I'll try."

The low dawn light intermingled with the glow from the fireplace. The group held hands and chanted in foreign words.

Cold and tired didn't begin to describe his physical shape and his mental state wasn't any better. His patience was nonexistent. He leaned toward Richard. "I'll give you about two seconds to tell me what the fuck is going on."

"Come with me into the kitchen."

Richard poured two cups of coffee and handed one to him. "As you know, Peyton is a victim of black magic and they're driving out the powers that are killing her." Richard gulped the hot liquid. "The long story. When Vadoma contacted me, I thought she'd lost her marbles. Jillian spoke to the old woman and

71

believed her. The short of it. Could they harm Peyton any more than you having her out all night?"

"You bastard." Cole threw his mug in the sink.

A wrenching cry wailed from the great room. "That's Peyton." He spun intent on rescuing her from the circus of freaks. Richard tackled him and restrained him on the floor. "Ugh."

In a wrestling maneuver, Cole twisted and had Richard at the disadvantage. His brother-in-law lay on his back. Cole immobilized Richard's shoulders with his knees and sat on his chest. Cole heaved in a breath, cocked his fist back.

"Don't do something you'll regret." Jill's calm voice resonated inside his head, and pleaded for rationale.

He halted. "Give me one damn good reason."

Jilly whispered, "Bad karma. If you deck Richard, Hendricks will cull your negative energy and use it against Peyton. It's as simple as that. Peyton is hanging on by a thread, don't give him more ammunition to hurt her."

With every heartbeat, Cole's head pounded and wanted to kick the shit out of somebody. Anybody. And he had Richard in his grasp. Cole closed his eyes, focusing on Peyton. He lowered his arm, scrambled off of Richard and helped him up. He'd lost his sanity for a split second. "I'm tired, worried…Sorry man, I didn't mean to take it out on you…but don't you ever tackle me like that again because next time, I won't stop."

Cole pivoted to Jillian. "Start talking."

After Peyton's screams abated, Jillian's hand spanned across her waist offering him and Richard seats at the kitchen table. Once everyone settled, her mouth opened then closed. She took a deep breath. "Hendricks initiated this black magic if you will. Vadoma, as her name means, is an all knowing one and came to free Peyton of the sorcerers' spell by interlacing her spirit with Peyton's."

Cole rolled his eyes. Jilly spoke to two men who lived their lives by logic. "To begin with, how did this Vadoma know about Peyton's problems, or for that matter how does this strange woman think she can overcome Hendricks?"

"Vadoma caught a glimpse of Peyton driving home. She saw Peyton doubled over from stomach pains and used telepathy to journey into Peyton's body and soul discovering her problem. She traveled though Peyton's mind to the memory area of her brain and found us."

"You're kidding right?" Cole rubbed his eyebrow.

"I try not to think about what she saw you two doing." Jillian laughed

"Jill, you're off track again." Richard shook his head.

Jillian cleared her throat. "Anyway, I gave Vadoma permission to come...and...try to save Peyton. Hendricks is attaching to Peyton two ways, physically and mentally."

"I'll try anything to save Peyton."

Peyton shrieked again.

Cole rose. "But it sounds like they're killing her."

Jilly grasped his arm and tugged him back to his seat. "Give them a chance."

Several hours later, Vadoma entered the kitchen. "That Hendricks is a strong one. He fought us the entire time. We know where he is. He used a possession as a talisman. If you want Peyton to survive, take it away from him."

Chapter Ten

Cole adjusted the hard-plated, reinforced vest that included ballistic shoulder and side protection. The policeman from one of the tactical hostage rescue units gave him a combat helmet too. What in the world did he get himself into? He was an attorney who sat at a desk for most of his waking hours. Yes, he worked out, but there was a hell of a difference. The punching bag never hit back and the exercise equipment damn sure didn't try to murder him.

Captain Lewinski jostled his right arm. "I don't like you being here, but you've got friends in higher places than I do. Don't get in our way or God forbid killed. The paperwork would be horrendous."

"I'll try my best." Cole's middle finger itched to raise Lewinski's rank from Captain to a full bird colonel, but instead he repositioned the cumbersome covering.

"The infrared heat signatures suggest he's in that building. When I give the signal, follow Porter." The commander indicated one of the three men leaning against a concrete wall. Lewinski crouched low and dashed to a van disguised as the local utility company's repair truck.

Pungent odors wafted past Cole's nose and the stench didn't come from the dumpster he peered around to scan the bricked street. The run-down warehouse district in Courtney, Colorado housed transients, druggies and prostitutes, and the majority of buildings had broken glass panes. According to the intel, at this very moment, most of the structures were vacant except for the one adjacent to him.

Vadoma gave Hendricks' whereabouts, but not the exact location, and cautioned that he might have another captive, possibly more. The old woman had been unsure because there were two trustworthy souls that comingled with hers, a motherly spirit and a child.

A youngster in the hands of Hendricks pissed Cole off. Captain Lewinski was correct. He had made several telephone calls and used every marker to force his way into this rescue operation. The men didn't like the idea of a greenhorn in their midst, because he was a liability. But Cole had been adamant to catch the son of a bitch who caused so much pain and torment to Peyton and other women.

Porter whistled. After his fingers walked, he aimed his thumb over his shoulder indicating the entrance Lewinski spoke about earlier.

Cole dipped his chin to acknowledge the man, but something didn't feel right. Even though, the captain had state of the art equipment, Cole would defy the commander's orders and follow his gut instinct. He waited until the squad infiltrated the site where the heat signature traced a human figure then darted to another.

This particular building called to him. He couldn't describe the sensation zinging through him, but he recognized a consciousness begging for help and a heart that cried for healing. Is this what his sisters felt?

Jillian had been open and discussed her gift. She told him he had it also, but he never believed her, until now. Maybe these manifestations originated from their mother leaving, and as children they wanted the relief of the ache that burdened them. "No way." Although after what he had seen the past couple of months, there could be some truth to the subject.

Cole shook his head and stared at a dilapidated entry. He grabbed the handle, twisted, and shoved. The rickety door fell off the hinges and crashed to the cement floor, launching a cloud of dust. "Damn." The booming echoes faded while dirt floated in the air. As gravity took over, the rays of sunlight coming through the window's openings highlighted their fall.

He withdrew his firearm and sneaked down the hallway. The crunch of glass under his steel-toed boots sounded like the explosions from IED's. Every little noise seemed to amplify ten times its true decibel level. He hesitated and angled his head around the first threshold on the right. He peered inside a chamber. Nothing. He eyed another exposed area several feet to his left and carefully headed toward it.

Within his soul, pain and anguish burned. How did he know that Hendricks was close? He swallowed hard, readied his handgun, and burst into the room.

A bound and very pregnant woman screamed around the gag. Tears flowed down both of her cheeks and dropped to her bloodied shirt.

"Shut up, bitch." Hendricks placed a knife to her protruding abdomen. The edge of the blade indented her stomach.

Wow, Vadoma was correct. There were two. And Cole not only heard the mom, but the baby's distress too.

"Drop your weapon." Cole raised the bead on the

end of the barrel until it centered on Hendricks' forehead.

"Not a chance. I'll slice her open before you squeeze the trigger, and she'll bleed to death."

"You ready to test your theory? I am." Cole hoped his bluff worked.

Hendricks' wild eyes flitted from side to side like a feral animal caught in a poacher's cage. Seconds later, his demeanor changed, and his gaze transformed into defiance. "By the way, how's Peyton doing?"

"You son-of-a-bitch." Cole's hatred emerged, and he wanted to kill the sorry excuse for a man. *That's what Hendricks' wants.* He remembered what Jillian had said and exhaled through his nose, erased any negative emotions, and stepped closer to his target.

"Did you honestly think that old Romanian woman would be able to stop me?" Hendricks' sneered.

"I don't know what you're talking about." Cole shuffled toward the killer.

"Stop." Hendricks doubled over and dropped his knife. "Ahh, the bitch is back."

Cole kicked the blade out of the way and quickly brought his weapon back to Hendricks' head.

Hendricks snatched a shard of jagged glass and lunged toward the woman.

Cole dived for Hendricks and stretched. Time rippled into an eternity. Would he make it in time to save the hostage or would he fail and watch her die? Death had a unique odor. After a case led him to Iraq and Afghanistan, he never wanted to smell the casualties of war again.

Cole snagged Hendricks' forearm and tackled him to the floor. He shot a quick glimpse to the woman.

"Run. There are police officers outside." Out of the corner of his eye, Cole glanced at Hendricks' captive struggling to move within the confines of her bound ankles. While hobbling across the room, she whimpered and disappeared through the door. Relieved she made it out, Cole relaxed.

Hendricks rolled, taking Cole with him.

"Enough of this shit." Cole wrestled Hendricks until he was on top of the maniac. He pounded his fist into the psycho's face. Hendricks' body went limp. Cole scrutinized the serial killer. Hendricks wasn't the bad ass anymore, and he'd personally see to it that this guy would never harm another woman again.

"We'll take it from here." Captain Lewinski holstered his gun.

Cole rose. "I expected more resistance."

"I've seen many reactions, but you never can guess which ones you'll come across." The commander loosened his helmet strap.

"Well, I'm not through with him." Cole reared his foot back and rammed the tip of the steel-toes into Hendricks' ribs. "That's for Peyton." He launched another kick. "And that's for all the women who died by your filthy hands." Cole dispensed one more. "That's from me, you slimy bastard." Hendricks' bones crackled, and he groaned.

"Damn it." Lewinski seized Cole by the shoulder. "Get out of here." The commander's head tilted toward the entrance.

Porter rushed into the room. "Captain, do you need help?"

"We'll need an ambulance." He cleared this throat. "Hendricks fell."

Porter perused the area. "From what?"

"Not from, to. I've never seen anyone more inept at balance in all my life."

"Yeah, right. What am I to put in my report?" Porter questioned the commander.

"Exactly what you saw. I'll detail the rest prior to you coming in."

Cole regarded Lewinski and nodded once. "If you need anything at all, Captain, you know where to find me."

Chapter Eleven

A week later, Cole stood outside the hospital room. Peyton's, Jillian's, and Leah's laughter echoed into the hallway. He smiled.

The detectives had called him with news of Hendricks' new home. He was institutionalized with an IQ level of a five-year-old. When he had jumped Hendricks, Vadoma knew Cole was in trouble and helped by incapacitating Hendricks. While the old woman had control over the psycho, she bestowed a special gift especially made for the murderer. Cole chuckled. Old Vadoma kicked his mental ass.

There was something else happening that gave him the willies. He shuddered. The doctors couldn't explain why, but Hendricks was learning at an exceptional rate.

Cole sighed. He wouldn't worry about that now. Kevin had told him Hendricks wouldn't stand trial, but would be incarcerated for the rest of his life. The son-of-a-bitch deserved to have more punishment meted out, but as long as Peyton was comfortable with the circumstances, he was a happy man.

He ambled inside as Jillian and Leah gave Peyton a kiss on the cheek. Leah whispered in Peyton's ear, and Peyton's cheeks changed to a vermillion hue.

"Glad to see my bright-shining star is getting out today." His fingers tightened into a fist and held the answer to all their questions. "The detectives found this."

Peyton gasped. "The bracelet you gave to me that I lost at the conference in New Orleans. Wait. It looks different."

"It is. Hendricks found this and used it against us. Vadoma added some crystals. Her group initiated a cleansing ceremony and finished with a blessing. I had the clasp reworked." He chose not to tell Peyton and scare her with what the old woman had warned. In the near future, they would be calling Vadoma again.

Peyton offered her wrist.

For the second time, he fastened the beautiful piece on his bright-shining star. "I have one request."

"Sure, what is it?" Peyton's head tilted a little to the side. Her smile reached her eyes, which gave him the strength to forge ahead.

He gathered Peyton's hands in his. "Will you marry me and be the mother of my children?"

Tears erupted and streamed down her face. "Yes, I want nothing more than to be by your side for as long as we live."

God, he loved this woman.

Epilogue

One year later

"In the bed, now. Doctor's orders not mine." Cole whisked the covers back and helped Peyton lay down.

"I'm expecting, not an invalid." She nestled under the blankets he drew to her non-existent waistline. "A beached whale, maybe, but not an invalid."

He thought it best to not comment on her 'beached whale' reference. "Promise me you'll rest a couple of hours."

"Cross my heart… Hey," She entwined her fingers with his, "I'm glad you forgave your mom and invited her to be part of our lives, especially now. It meant a lot to her and me."

"Yeah? Me too. It's hard to explain. I have a peace I never thought I'd have."

"I can see the difference. Your eyes radiate the inner peace you feel, and your whole demeanor has changed. It's not you against the world anymore and… Anyway, I'm delighted for you and us. By the way, have you thought of any names for our son and daughter? Most people have already decided by this time." Peyton released him and snuggled under the quilt.

"I'll be happy with whatever you choose. As long as they are healthy. Let's talk about it later." By the time he kissed Peyton's cheek, she had dozed off.

He crept out of the room and closed the door.

Jillian insisted they stay at the cabin so they could supervise the crews building their new house, but he knew his sister. She wanted to be a part of their pregnancy, and he didn't blame her one bit.

He had stowed most of his belongings in storage and moved Peyton's things. He wanted the love of his life to feel at home surrounded by her sentimental items.

Watching the babies grow in Peyton had a profound effect on him from the very beginning. Instead of Peyton getting morning sickness, he did. When it came to nesting, he couldn't seem to get the cabin clean enough to suit him, and he'd bet he ate more antacids than Captain Lewinski's entire team.

The phone rang from the guest bedroom he'd converted into his office. The sound reminded him of the downside of locating his law practice in town. He'd been training a new legal secretary, and the graduate waiting to take his bar exam, which turned out perfect for him. Peyton had reservations about finding two people fitting his exact needs, but he'd attributed her concerns to rampant hormones careening through her system.

Giving the green light for his new employees to contact him here allowed him to stay at home and keep Peyton off her feet. He checked the caller id and snatched the receiver from its cradle. "Graham, how can I help you?"

His associate ended the rather lengthy explanation, most newbies had a tendency to expound until his eyes crossed. He should be used to it, but at times... "No problem, fax the contract over to me, and I'll take a look at it."

"Cole?" Peyton's tone didn't sound right. What was she doing out of bed and in the living room?

"Graham, I'll talk to you later." Cole hung up.

He sprinted toward Peyton's voice. She stood by the door with the overnight bag slung over her shoulder.

"It's time." The twinkle in her eyes unleashed an avalanche of pride for the love of his life. Very soon, she would deliver a family, and he couldn't wait to meet their babies.

"Let's go." He grabbed the keys and her weekend satchel then helped Peyton into the car.

After he cranked the engine, he gazed into her eyes. A special sparkle illuminated from them. "Have I told you today how much I love you?"

"If you don't count the ones every half hour since we awakened, but I like hearing you say the words." She closed the distance between them and kissed him.

His stomach muscles contracted. He broke into a sweat and ended their connection. "Ah. Damn that hurts. Your labor pains are killing me. If it was physically possible for men to have kids, I wouldn't." Cole shifted to drive and gunned the accelerator.

"That's why women have children."

"And that's why I'll let you." Cole winked at her as she settled against the leather seat. A powerful and undeniable thought occurred to him; children offered hope to adults that life will continue even when faced with the atrocities in this world, including people like Hendricks. Unlike Hendricks' victims, he and Peyton were blessed by beginning a new chapter. He was one lucky man.

An excerpt of
Walking Into Her Heart

by

Susan JP Owens

A First Realm Novel

Walking Into Her Heart

Cover Art by *Diana Carlile*

The Wild Rose Press, Inc.
PO Box 708
Adams Basin, NY 14410-0708
Visit us at www.thewildrosepress.com

Publishing History
First Faery Rose Edition, 2013
Print ISBN 978-1-62830-068-0
Digital ISBN 978-1-62830-069-7

A First Realm Novel
Published in the United States of America

Dedication

To my fellow author,
Nese Lane,
who "walked" every footfall with me.

~

And to my husband and "Soul Mate,"
Jimmy,
for his love and unwavering support.

Acknowledgments

This particular novel took a tribe that I'd like to acknowledge for their technical help, valuable resources and information: Captain H.D. "Dusty" Spain; John St. Germain, Operations Manager, Jackson Hole Aviation; LtCol. Wren Meyers, USMCR (Ret); Sergeant Kim Wolff, TPD; Megan Gersbach, PA; Nancy Livingston; Judy Juergens; Margaret Wilson; Pat Holloway; Keith Moninger; Martha Tutor; Gina Veillon; Jodi Fields; Margaret Bryant; Cindy Schleede; Jake D., and the members of the Heart of Texas, RWA chapter. A special thank you and kudos to my editor, Ally, and cover artist, Diana.

Chapter One

Columbia, South America—Ten Years Earlier

Kyle Pressley scrubbed a hand over his face as he led his team through the thick jungle north of the Ecuadorian border. His beard and mustache itched. Sweat trickled down his back, the salt stinging the mosquito and God only knew what other bites. He gulped the sultry air. Damn, the humidity made it difficult to breathe and clung to everything including his weapon. He swiped his palm down one thigh then the other. The acrid smell of the lab one klick south hovered with no breeze to carry away the fucking obnoxious odor.

The two-by-ten-foot boards settled in the mud marked the path to one of the biggest known cocaine work-camps. Once the team found the site's position, they were to reconnoiter, then provide GPS coordinates, but not engage. His superiors wanted any shipments tracked to the drug cartel's new mode of transportation, a submarine. Their intel had been based on a paid informant, and he hoped like hell this wasn't some wild goose chase.

He set a parallel course to the planks, hacking his way through the dense undergrowth. His instincts howled. Adrenaline shot through his system. The hair on his neck rose. His gut wrenched. He stilled. Catching movement to his left, he clenched his fist and held his arm up to call a halt to his team, then melded by a tree.

The Assistant Secretary had asked his SEAL team to try out the new video gear, including a screen detailing each member's position and point of view in real time. The usual load-outs used for this type of assignment went back to basics, a machete and a mere compass because of the rain forest's impenetrable canopy.

His team had practiced for several months before testing the advanced equipment in a live situation. The special rig was integrated into their helmets and pierced the jungle's substantial covering. All he had to do was think which team member's POV he wanted, and the images would appear on one of the screens. Processing what he was seeing on both displays and multi-tasking his thoughts, the high stimulus caused his brain to seize, which changed the screen to snow. The innovators had called it a white-out. His team called it something else. "Did you see it?"

"Affirmative," Dan's voice whispered through his ear piece. "I have a bad feeling."

He did too.

Kyle had joined the Navy and risen through the ranks at breakneck speed. Dan, nearly a decade his senior, had become his mentor. Together, their team was a force to be reckoned with. He'd declined a vote of his constituents to join SEAL Team VI. Those men were the elite, intelligent, had guts, courage, and were bound together by one hell of a brotherhood. He'd been honored, but he didn't see himself doing this for another ten years, and he sure as hell wanted to see his thirtieth birthday.

Bark chipped off the tree above his head. Kyle counted until he heard the gunfire report. The guerrillas had exposed their position. He dropped to the ground, using the thick trunk as protection. Bullets sprayed where his chest and face had been seconds before.

Out of the corner of his eye, he caught an asshole trying to hide. He double tapped. His target crumbled.

The barrage of lethal ammo flew by his head while shredding nearby foliage.

"Jesus Christ, engage the fucking bastards," he yelled while he squeezed the trigger, inundating the area with lead. The hail of gunfire rose close to Dan's position.

"Two?"

"A little bit busy right now. Ahh!"

"Fuck this shit." Kyle snatched a grenade, pulled the pin, and threw. "Fire in the hole!"

The eerily quiet minutes that followed slithered into what seemed an eternity. Kyle spoke into his mic. "Red One here."

"Red Three."

"Red Four."

"Red Five."

He waited. "Two?" Kyle eyed Dan's video feed. All he saw was snow-fucking-white.

"Red Three to One. I'm looking at Two, and he's down."

Kyle's right lens picked up Two's position and Three's image. "I see him. On my way. Secure the perimeter."

He backtracked and spotted Dan's body, lying at an odd angle. He knelt beside Dan. His severed femoral artery spurted blood with each heartbeat. "Stay with me. We'll get you out of here." He swallowed the lump in his throat and applied a tourniquet then compressed the wound.

Kyle keyed his mic. "One to Three, request medevac." His neutral voice belied the urgency screaming through his gut.

Dan's eyes opened. "I'm done...go."

"Don't be a dickhead, Forbes. Remember when you were stabbed last year? The knife had pierced your lung and you pulled through." Kyle tore the corner of a packet and sprinkled the blood clotting agent. Every man on his team had medical training. Their lives depended on it.

"Leave, prick. Fuck me, that shit burns." Dan winced.

"Stop being a pussy and grow some balls. You've survived worse." His injury was life threatening. Dan might have a chance based on a few things going his way, like an extraction—stat—a little help from lady luck, and a damn strong conviction to live. But Dan acted like he didn't care if he lived or died.

Dan groaned. "I don't want to."

"What? Why?" Fuck, he never expected Dan to give up, not this fast. This wasn't the man he knew and admired. No matter what team a man was on, they were bad asses to the end, especially when the damage had been caused by the cock sucking enemy. A SEAL lived just to piss them off. And each man faced death, head-on.

"None of your business."

"Pull your head out of your ass." Kyle swallowed hard, fearing the worst. He wouldn't let Dan concede, not on his watch. He had to figure out what was going on.

Kyle closed his eyes to journey into Dan's mind. He concentrated on his spiritual self, some call it the third eye, but he preferred to think of it as a portal. While clearing negative energy, Kyle released his physical form and embraced his spirit. He had been given the gift and the name Mind-Walker, which was one of the reasons he had excelled working with the new military equipment and had been chosen as the team leader.

Traveling to other realms was different than journeying into people's minds. In most instances, he had to cloak his presence, but not this time. He wanted Dan to know he was there and pushed his positive consciousness within Dan's. Dan's physical pain struck Kyle like a freight train. Kyle's leg throbbed. He blocked the excruciating agony and opened to his best friend's thoughts. Dan's memories flashed before him. Both of Dan's children, Aaron and Katherine jumping into their father's arms, happy their dad came home. Kyle was Aaron and Katherine's godfather, and he loved these kids as if they were his own. Another recollection unfolded before Kyle, Dan's wife smiled, then betrayal and heartbreak.

"You bastard, you're mind walking. You told me this was a bunch of bullshit."

"Would you have believed me?" This was the first time he had walked in Dan's mind and he opted not to veil his presence. Not too many people understood his ability and the ones that had… No. He didn't want to go there…Ever again.

Dan chuckled then grimaced. *"No. What happens if you're still here when I die?"*

Kyle discerned his best friend's life slipping away, the lack of oxygenated blood damaging Dan's heart as his will to survive diminished. *"When did Becca ask for a divorce?"*

Mail call...two days ago. I can't live without her, man."

"You should've told me...Don't give up...For your kids."

"She wants custody...Taking them on her symphony tours...Hiring a tutor."

Kyle willed his strength to Dan. *"Stay with me...We'll fight this together...I'll help you...I've means."*

"I know who you are, prick."

"Then you know I can hire the best damn attorneys money can buy and we'll win."

"Will you look after them?"

Dan's energy and light faded with each breath. Frustration seared every neurological wave. Why couldn't he change Dan's outlook, make a difference? *"I'll make sure the twins will want for nothing, but you can give them more than I can, by staying alive, being their dad, watching them grow up, graduate, get married and have your grandchildren."*

"Tired...Cold."

The love Dan had for his wife and children rendered Kyle silent. His heart ached for his buddy. He pleaded, not only for Dan's family, but for him too. *"Don't do this."*

Dan heaved a sigh. *"Tell Aaron, Kat, and Becca, I love them."*

"I will." Kyle drew on his own energy, expounding further to his surroundings. *"Hang on."*

Still not enough, he expanded to cull the positive forces in the sky, space, then the universe. *"Stay with me."* Kyle called on his spirit guides and the angels for their help.

Dan gurgled, *"Please go."*

"No, I need you to live." Kyle gathered all the lifesaving influences and launched the potent power into Dan. *"Come on."* Kyle filled his lungs and released the life giving oxygen to Dan by telepathy. *"Fuck, fight damn it."*

"No more, let me go."

Kyle stilled then honored Dan's last request and walked out.

"So damn cold."

He gathered Dan in his arms keeping him warm in the hundred-plus temperature. "I love you, man."

Dan nodded. "Me too." Then he was gone.

Tears blurred Kyle's vision. "Fuckin' A." If he'd known about Becca's letter, he would've kept Dan from this mission. He would take the responsibility to tell the twins their father had died, on his watch.

For the first time and when it counted most, he'd been unable to make a difference mind walking. If he was incapable of accomplishing such a simple task as to help Dan live for his children, then what good was his gift from the First Realm? He managed to have the right stuff for covert operations, slip in the enemy's head and step out without them knowing he'd been there. Hell, he could plant ideas into the fucker's subconscious, and they'd believed it was theirs. He'd had saved numerous agents from certain death and gave up the positions of the rogues who'd put them there. How had he failed to keep Dan alive?

A hand on his shoulder jostled him. "We found the camp several meters west, and everyone scattered. I've sent the coordinates. They're on their way…Pressley, give Forbes to me. We need to get the hell out of here."

"Fuck off." He hoisted Dan over his shoulder and carried him to the helo rendezvous.

With each step, his desolation grew. His heart ripped in two, then fragmented into tiny pieces. He cursed. The loss of Dan was like a death of a brother.

His brother.

They were trained in stealth, movement, and extraction. This mission was supposed to be a cakewalk, new equipment tests, keeping undercover, not engaging. The worst part, this job was their last. Kyle had planned a vacation with Dan and his twins. He should've keyed in when Becca wasn't able to join them.

He sighed. Dan was going home all right, in a damn body bag. He had screwed up as the team leader, and the hardest fact he had to accept, he failed Aaron and Katherine. Not only them, but also, his spirit guides, the First Realm, and his ability to help his world when needed.

The rotor wash whipped from the black hawk, lowering to the ground. He climbed in. When the medic stretched to take Dan's lifeless form, Kyle growled. Dan's blood covered him, some of it still tacky, some of it dried. The coppery smell filtered to his nostrils. Life had always been uncertain in their line of work. He sure as hell expected more from himself.

He had a duty to Dan. Aaron and Katherine would have everything…except a dad. All the hurt and anguish boiled inside his gut and the repulsive mixture spilled to every part of him including his soul. He had pledged to use his ability for good without undermining destiny. Did he really think he could change Dan's outlook, snatch his best friend from death's clutches, and alter fate? The simple answer was yes. He held himself accountable and vowed never to use his gift again.

Chapter Two

The First Realm
Present Day

"You have done well, but you need help," One-Who-Soars-With-Eagles communicated telepathically to Tim.

The aura surrounding the medicine man's spirit demanded his attention. "I don't want Shelby to die like I did."

The bell tinkled as his wife left the book store. From above and within the First Realm, Tim watched with the shaman. The sun bathed Shelby's skin and the golden highlights of her brown hair shimmered. He longed to touch the silken shafts, her soft skin, to walk hand-in-hand. He'd give anything to make love to her one more time.

One-Who-Soars-With-Eagles' methodical cadence dissolved his thoughts. "Observing her struggle is difficult."

Shelby's tireless effort to find his murderer put her in danger. Why hadn't he told her? Taken the time to share with her about the fetish, the exposure, and risks involved with the Kachina doll? Now in this so-called afterlife, he was forced to accept the medicine man's plan. Even if it meant an eternal damnation from the First Realm, he wanted Shelby safe, happy on earth, and a kinder death than his.

"However, she is the key," One-Who-Soars-With-Eagles continued. "We can guide her much like we directed you."

Tim's guttural laugh stung with distaste. "You helped me? Based on where I'm standing, she doesn't have a chance." Having to follow the shaman's divine guidance disgusted him. He preferred intervention, but had no choice.

"There's more at stake than your woman's life. Potent powers are within Ten-Blue-Sun. Little-Dove-Feathers must have possession of the doll, for she will know how to harness the energy to win the upcoming battles and heal the scars. Shelby is an important step. Dangerous entities will be countering our efforts not only on Earth but here too. When the baby is born, we will have a chance to right all the wrongs."

"Shelby's going to have a...babe?" Mixed emotions inundated him, the light of Tim's spirit dimmed. He understood One-Who-Soars-With-Eagles. This wasn't an immaculate conception. Shelby would have a lover, a partner...or a husband.

"Her life's path is crucial."

"Let me get this straight. You used me and now you want to take advantage of Shelby too, all for a damn doll and a baby who's not born yet?"

"You'll learn many things in our spirit world, but first, your wife must release you."

Tim peered down on Mother Earth while Shelby window shopped. He would bet she wasn't ready to let him go. For that matter, he wasn't either. Now, when they were together, she'd talk to him for hours and he'd answer the only way he knew how. He had discovered how to bundle his energy to communicate through physical means, to grasp, to blow wisps of air, and he reveled in Shelby's presence.

To acquire the skill of manifestation was a long process. But he had wanted, no, needed to seek out his soul mate. He was pleased Shelby never feared his spiritual existence.

The first several times were tough. She'd cried at the injustice. But her perseverance and resolve prevailed. She had made several promises to him, to find out who murdered him and never marry again. Pledges he wasn't sure she should keep. He'd have a hell of a time getting her to break those oaths. Between the medicine man and him, they could influence Shelby to find his killer and whatever else, the shaman had up his proverbial sleeve, but until the baby was born, their powers were limited, only to navigate, not intervene.

Maybe she would find someone, a friend, one who wouldn't be threatened by her strengths and her strong sense of commitment. He vowed if the right man entered her life, he'd give Shelby his blessing. For now, he'd have to take the only course available to him, to follow the shaman.

One-Who-Soars-With-Eagles' whispered, "Good, I'm glad you have come to this conclusion. When Shelby releases you, you'll be able to go on to your next step and receive more power for our war. Shelby's spirit guide will take over and assist."

The medicine man's next words brooked no argument. "Come. We have many things to do, many levels to complete."

Chapter Three

4th of July - Jackson, WY

When Shelby Littleton caught a glimpse of the ice cream parlor, her mouth watered. The icy treat promised a reprieve. She'd take a short cut through the town square where the tall trees and evergreens would provide shade.

A humming sound buzzed around her. The cool clasp of her husband's hand on her elbow reassured her. "Tim, I have a feeling our Kachina doll has more history than my research has unfolded, but I intend to learn everything I can. My gut feeling tells me you were murdered for her. Babe, you've never left my side and I'll always be grateful." Air brushed over her ear giving his approval.

Even though she'd much rather have her husband's physical presence, she would take any form of him. At first, she thought she was losing her mind, but now, she'd accepted his corporeal death, her earthly life without him, and his spirit. Her first call of business was to find her husband's murderer.

A sudden noise came from her right. She stilled, tilting her head away from the buzz of the cars and people. There it was again, a whine. Cautiously, she pursued the sound. A poor dog ensnared in twine, cowered on his belly. She crept forward and dropped to her knees. The canine shied from her. Shelby's eyes connected with its dark brown ones quieting his cries.

"You're scared. Why don't you have a collar?" She stretched to stroke him, her efforts rewarded when he offered his floppy ears. "Let's try to find an end. How did the rope get so tangled, huh?" He nosed her and allowed her help.

"Give me a little more time, I can't find the beginning. "Roll over on your side. Good baby. What do you know, you're a girl."

The high pitched frequency associated with her husband's spirit screeched. "Tim, what are you trying to tell me?"

"Pardon me?"

In her peripheral vision, she glimpsed a pair of tanned cowboy boots stopping alongside her.

"Looks like you could use an extra hand."

His baritone voice ignited tingles down her arms and resonated to her fingertips. Shelby's gaze hooked onto his mahogany eyes. Her mouth opened to answer but nothing came. Sable brown hair brushed the starched collar and his square jaw sported a five o'clock shadow even though it was just past noon. The corner of his lips inched higher transforming into a smile sending warm sensations to her belly then lowered to her feminine folds.

"Here, let me." He retrieved a penknife out of his pocket and knelt beside her. "Hold tight. I don't want the dog to move and get cut with my blade."

She nodded, forming the words to thank him, but her jaw quivered. She clamped her lips together. Goosebumps rose over her skin. She stared at his deft fingers, full of strength as they gently finessed the rope loose. Now free, the canine jumped onto Shelby's lap taking every inch.

The handsome man sat on his haunches, leveled his luscious gaze with hers and chuckled. "I think you found a friend."

Her id swung into action along with her body. The ripples of pleasure aroused her in places where only her husband had given her full satisfaction. Shocked by her response, she processed her reaction. Since Tim's death, her desire for physical release or emotional attachment had been nonexistent. Who was this guy?

He shucked off his hat, gliding his hand through the thick locks of hair. "Can I help you with her?"

His eyes shined with life. She couldn't break their contact, didn't want to, but in the end, she shook off the moment, ending the connection.

This time her voice didn't falter. "I guess I should find a shelter and see if anyone claims her."

The cowboy settled the Stetson on his head. "I happen to know of one down the street. It's within walking distance. I'll show you. Can you coax her off your lap?"

Shelby relaxed her grip guiding the dog up on all fours. "Thanks."

The gentleman helped her to stand. "My name is Kyle. What's yours?"

As she stood, she wobbled. "Shelby. Nice to meet you."

He steadied her. "Same here." His words were sincere, then his gaze turned introspective.

"Is something wrong? Kyle?"

"No, ma'am…this way." He gestured with his arm.

She quickened her stride to walk beside him. The

cool shadows gave way to sunlight while she coaxed the dog to follow.

They approached a cross walk where a group of older women waited for the signal light to change.

A single voice rose above the din. "My dear, how are you today?"

Kyle panned to the right, searching, and then smiled. "Well, Mrs. Dent, I'm doing just fine. How are you?" He waited for Mrs. Dent as she shuffled through the ladies.

Her sun bonnet bounced with each word she spoke, "I'm doing well. We've missed you at our bridge tournaments, but most of all, I miss my partner. We always won and I don't take too kindly to losing."

Kyle nodded. "I've been out of town on business."

Mrs. Dent's alert eyes landed on her and the dog. "Looks like you're busy. Spreading yourself too thin isn't good for you."

"Yes, ma'am, you're right. This is Shelby. Shelby, Mira Dent." The signal changed and Kyle extended his arm. "May I help you, Mira?"

"I'd like that. Shelby, nice to meet you." Mira grasped Kyle's elbow.

"Nice to meet you, also." Shelby lagged a few paces behind, instantly liking the spritely woman.

Mira shuffled with a slow gait and resumed her conversation with Kyle. "Please come and see me sometime. I miss your mom and dad. Tell your brother he's invited too. We can reminisce about old times." Mrs. Dent grasped Kyle's forearm for his support and stepped up onto the sidewalk, then released him. "Thank you. Kyle, you don't have to be a stranger. I know we miss our loved ones, but we shouldn't be remiss and forget them."

He kissed her cheek. "My pleasure…You've always been thoughtful of my family. I'll take you up on your offer and bring something for that sweet tooth of yours."

Her smile brightened. "I'll have the tea ready."

Kyle straightened and winked. "I'll look forward to it. You take care now."

Mira's head bobbed. "You know I always do."

Kyle had extended kindness to his lovely friend. Surprisingly, his strong body adapted to guide Mira with gentleness.

"She seems like a very sweet woman."

His focus hinted he was a thousand miles away, then his awareness returned. "She is."

****

Shelby grinned at how the young and vivacious veterinarian's assistant greeted them with a pleasant smile. "Mr. Pressley, what can I do for you today?"

He held the door open while Shelby entered coaxing her four-legged friend inside.

Kyle wiped his boots on the entry rug. "Hi Liz, I see you have volunteered for holiday pay."

Liz's expressive face amplified her jovial attitude. "Oh yeah, several of us did."

Kyle removed his hat. "I appreciate everyone's dedication. The reason we're here, has anyone been looking for a lost dog? We found this one downtown."

Liz peered at a list hanging on the wall. "Give me a moment to check."

When Shelby sat in the closest vinyl covered chair, the canine scampered over and nuzzled her thigh. She stroked the red coat. The dog's brown eyes fasten with hers as though she was trying to tell her something. Although, Shelby didn't understand her, she did discern one thing. She had a connection with the brown-eyed renegade.

Liz poked her head over the counter. "Nope."

Kyle's hand whisked through his hair. "Is there a vacant kennel available?"

Shelby vaulted from her seat. "No. I mean, until someone comes forward, I'll keep her."

Liz's calm voice echoed in the room, "This facility is a no-kill-animal shelter, compliments of Mr. Pressley here, if that helps."

"How nice." That sounded tongue-in-cheek, she rephrased. "Truly, that's terrific. Do you think you'd have time to bathe and groom her for me? Also, I'll give you my cell number, in case someone comes for her."

"Of course, I can have Delores start on her right now. Would you like to wait or come back?"

"I'll stay, thank you."

Kyle stepped beside her. "How about a cup of coffee? I'm buying."

Liz rounded into the reception area with a leash in her hands. "I just made a fresh pot. Let me have your new friend. I'll feed and water her for you too."

Kyle led the way into the cozy lunchroom. He directed her to sit while he poured the java and set the mug in front of her.

She raised her arm in a cheers salute. "Thanks. I needed this."

He joined her across the table. "Where are you from?"

She sipped the hot steaming liquid and set the drink

on a coaster. "Texas." Her to-do list seemed never ending, but the first item was to find her husband's killer. Would she be able to recognize the right clues, understand them, and devise a plan to catch the bad guys? Sure, no problem, she could become Sherlock Holmes or Hercule Poirot...fictional characters. Her stomach curdled.

Shelby remembered the next decision she had to make. Should she change Alessa's position to president? Her youngest sister ran the business with efficiency and her new marketing ideas had outstanding results. The old adage timing is everything still held true. She shook her head. Her mind drifted a lot lately. There were times when life and stress were overwhelming.

She sighed. "You?"

"Wyoming. Are you on vacation...maybe with your husband?"

He noticed my wedding band. "No, I'm widowed." Shelby glanced away. When would the pain stop and her heart feel whole again?

Kyle murmured, "I'm sorry."

She raised her eyes to meet his. No other man compared to her soul mate and his presence never wavered. She stilled. Except today when she met Kyle, Tim's spirit had been AWOL ever since. Her gaze pierced Kyle's, taking his measure. He didn't back down or blink. She gave in first and focused on his strong fingers wrapped around his cup. "Thank you. It's hard."

Kyle's whispered. "I'm sure it is." He cleared his throat. "Where in Texas do you live? It's a big state."

Shelby grinned. "Everything is bigger in Texas or

so the saying goes. The heart of Texas. How about you?"

"Near here…Are you enjoying your stay?"

"I am."

Kyle eased back in his chair. "So tell me, what have you seen?"

"Not a lot, been doing some research."

His eyebrows rose. "For what?"

"A book." She was here for research, just not her current work in progress—truth by omission. She didn't see a need to discuss her real task.

He angled forward. "What kind?"

"It's fiction." She hoped. The Kachina doll, known as Ten-Blue-Sun, had many powers for good, but her husband's death pointed to murder. She didn't have any evidence to take to the police. If she voiced her opinion, one of two things would happen. Either, she'd be branded a lunatic or her husband was a thief. As far as she was concerned, the latter didn't have merit. Tim had an exceptional moral standard.

Hell, when he drove, she'd cut her eyes to the speedometer, begging him to set the cruise control one mile per hour over the limit. He'd say, "Laws must be obeyed even if we don't agree with them." Nope, not him, no way would he have stolen anything.

"Is it about this area? I could help since I know most of the places around here."

"Thanks, but I shouldn't."

Kyle's head cocked. "Why not?"

"For many reasons. I don't know you for one." And second, for the first time since his death, Tim's presence left her. Third, she had to figure out the significance of the doll, and fourth, would she be killed

110

next?

A chuckle rumbled deep from within his broad chest. "If you let me help, we can get to know one another."

Her insides melted at the sound of his mirth. "Point taken. But what I need the most is a shower." She stood and washed her cup. "Do you want any more coffee?" She turned and met his gaze.

"I've had enough. Will you let me walk you to your hotel room?"

"No, you don't have to." She wiped the counter with the paper towel.

He rose from his chair. Reaching for the grounds to dump in the garbage, their hands met. "But I want to. I can help baby sit." Kyle nodded at the dog Delores had brought in a few minutes ago, now curled on the floor asleep. "Then, we could take in the fireworks, all three of us."

Her lower lip quivered from the jarring reaction of his touch. She gauged his character. His eyes shined with sincerity, his posture and manner open. She'd enjoy company who would actually talk back to her, unlike her conversations with Tim. As a local, he could possibly give her insight into the history of the Indian tribes.

The Kachina doll came from the Hopi people, but Tim wrote several unexplained entries in his journal pointing to the Shoshone and the Comanche. Through research she'd learned, the Shoshone language was a mixture of all three. She understood the connection with the Shoshone and the Comanche, but had questions concerning the Hopi lineage. She'd have to dig further.

Since she had met Kyle, Tim's spirit vanished. She didn't want to think about her husband leaving for good simply because she had male company. Her life hadn't been threatened since her arrival in Jackson, but her home had been burglarized several times. She weighed all the factors. "I'd like that."

Kyle winked. "We'll have a good time. Have you ever been to the Fourth celebration?"

"No, this will be my first time."

"You'll like it. I'll be waiting for you outside. I need to make a few phone calls."

After paying the bill and leaving her cell number with Liz, Shelby led them to her hotel. Out of the corner of her eye, she checked out Kyle. His stride gave him a self-confident air of command; she didn't think anyone would try to test him. For the first time since her husband died, she felt safe.

At the hotel door, she withdrew the keycard from her purse.

"I should check your room before you go in."

She added distance between them. "What? Why?"

If it were possible, he stood straighter, his chest heaved. The way he stated the words, "Anyone can get in your room" had more meaning than she could ascertain.

He strode inside and checked the premises. "All clear. I'll wait for you out on the porch."

****

As she closed the door, Kyle exhaled. Memories bombarded him. His dad sat him down with his brother, never shedding the tears that gathered in his eyes. 'I have bad news...Your mom didn't make it.' She'd been oblivious to her surroundings and men had kidnapped

112

her. They abducted her from her hotel, ending her life. He shook his head to end the foul flashback.

Kyle settled on the top of the wooden steps leading to her small veranda. The dog plopped down beside him. He wouldn't frighten Shelby with the dangers of keeping his company. Obligated for her protection, he made the appropriate phone calls to his security detail. Knowing he wouldn't see her again after the holiday, he opted not to tell her. Why invite questions?

If he were honest, there was something special about this gal. When he met her trying to free the dog, his gut rolled. Her bright eyes welcomed him. At that moment, he'd wanted to walk through her mind.

His gift had many benefits. The ability to journey into the recesses of someone's subconscious, to understand the person's intentions, gave him insights into their character and world. The pure of heart blessed him immeasurably. It always sounded corny even to him when he explained his experiences to his older brother, Jude. His sibling never believed in spirits or any other world except the one he was in.

At first, the lack of control bothered him. He'd project when he hadn't meant to do it. Through discipline and direction, astral projecting became manageable. By the time he'd mastered the power within, he'd kept the occurrences to himself. For the most part, people were good and decent. The evil ones...

Not many people could withstand the horror. His gut clenched, then churned with revulsion. He had first-hand knowledge of the heinous people walking this earth, corrupt perceptions of life left little doubt about their sanity.

During his military service, beyond enemy lines, he'd traveled into many adversarial minds. Appalled by the interrogation techniques inflicted upon prisoners of war, he'd sworn to help his fellow soldiers. Which he did with success, but his superiors used him unmercifully for other things. He'd saved lives, but many people benefited by prostituting his gift. After Dan died, he had kept his vow.

Kyle's insides roiled because he wanted to mind walk with Shelby. A woman he didn't know, a lady in all practicality he wouldn't see again, however, a soul he wished to visit.

He wanted her company. The challenge to get her to agree to watch the fireworks with him became paramount. In the break room when their hands met, the unexpected jolt traveled from his fingers through his body and landed on his third leg. He was an instant believer in the saying stiff as a fencepost. His groin tightened, again. As the evening progressed with Shelby, he'd know whether he was acting like an addled teenager or if his instinct was correct. He voted for the last.

Shelby stepped out of her room. He rose, and made modest adjustments. "Shall we go?" He gently tugged the leash. The sleeping dog yawned, then ambled to all fours and shook. "Little lady, you need to come with us."

"How do you think she'll react to the fireworks?" Shelby pursed her lips.

"We're about to find out. But I think she'll do fine."

At the town square, he led Shelby through a curved structure made of elk antlers held together by wire.

Once past the noted arch entrance, he guided her by the small of her back to a great view of the night sky.

****

The man glared into the lady's eyes, hoping to intimidate her. "How much are ya' talkin' about?" He didn't trust this one.

"Enough so you can have a fresh start…somewhere else."

He peered over the spectators to see Kyle and Shelby. "What about her?"

"If she gets in the way, deal with her."

He squinted, giving his evil look he practiced. "It'll cost ya' more."

"Just do the job correctly and you won't have any problems. But I understand what you want and agree to double the amount."

"You can count on it bein' done right." He laughed inwardly. His luck was changin'. He fixed his gaze on his paying customer ploddin' through the crowd. His tongue swiped across his lips. When he'd hesitated to take on Ms. Littleton, the ante upped immediately. He learnt that from his cousin playin' poker and it worked. Sweet vengeance, he'd be paid twice for the same job.

As for the wench on Kyle's arm, he'd already accepted that assignment. She'd be an easy target, unless she continued to hang with the asshole from the multi-millionaire's club. When the time was right, he'd play his hand.

Pressley had bodyguards. Ha! People thought he was stupid. He'd show them. Soon, the high and mighty Pressleys would be mournin'. He rubbed his hands together. Yep, an eye for an eye, that's what the good book says. A plum fact, hell is where he was headed, but he'd have plenty of money and fun getting there.

****

The hairs on the back of Kyle's neck rose. He shifted. Kyle widened his stance, balancing on the balls of his feet and searched the crowd noting first Shelby's position, then each group and person. No one stood out. His Navy SEAL training took over. Senses on high alert, he zeroed in on anything suspicious. His gut instinct kicked into gear, adrenaline coursed through his veins, his hands curled into fists at his side. His taut muscles readied for action.

He'd asked his two bodyguards to keep their distance so Shelby wouldn't question the need. *Shit*, if anything happened, he'd have to wing it until they could get across the square.

Hands grabbed his arm. Startled, he whirled to face his adversary, shoved his attacker back with one hand and cocked his arm to throw a haymaker. When he focused, Shelby stood in his grasp, her eyes rounded in horror. Anger gave way to relief. He captured her shoulder, tucked her to his side as he scanned the multitude of people. Not giving her a choice but to move with him, her arms wrapped around his waist while he circled, covering all three hundred and sixty degrees.

Her voice wavered, "My God, what's wrong?"

How would he explain the ominous instinct? He couldn't, but he understood something wasn't right. One of the many lessons he learned in the military, you act because by the time you react, it was too late. Another factor that was innate as breathing, assess the situation, then decide a course of action.

He glimpsed at the two men striding for him,

taking note everything was in order, he gave the sign and his bodyguards backed off.

As the youngest son of the Pressley empire, there were ups and downs living a privileged life. Money didn't make him any better than anyone else. The majority of occasions he felt luckier and other times, it was downright harder.

This was one of those instances. He didn't go around telling people he was worth a fortune, and as a newfound friend, he hadn't told Shelby. He expelled his breath and calmed.

"Nothing, we're good."

She hugged him and gazed into his eyes. The connection of her trust, coupled with his conviction to protect her, created an inconceivable force within him, producing a stimulus for something deeper, an impetus toward a commitment. He sucked in a breath and admitted there was more.

A visceral reaction drew him to her—where no woman had taken him in a long time. He visualized his hands in her thick brown hair spread on his pillows, tangled in sheets after a night in bed…with him. Sweet Jesus, it'd been ages since he'd had this type of response.

Her hazel eyes danced. Shelby tilted her head, and her silky hair cascaded down her back. The creamy skin of her neck invited him and his body answered in a primal way. His cock rose to the lure of her feminine appeal.

Her lips transformed into a beautiful smile and her natural beauty smacked him on target, and blood rushed to his dick. He shifted minimally to relieve the pressure in his jeans but not to dislodge her from his thigh. Hot streaks of desire shot through his veins, while tiny sparks set his skin on fire. He shivered, recognizing the irony. Reining in his thoughts, drawing back his fervor, he blinked long, inhaled fully and released the air. "When you touched my arm, I responded. I didn't mean to scare you." And he hadn't.

With Shelby's arms wrapped around his waist, their gazes still locked, her eyes were a window to her soul. He wanted to mind walk with Shelby. No. He intended to keep his vow. Damn, what was he thinking? What had this woman done to him? Or had he found a trustworthy lady? Everything was out of sync.

He had learned to listen to his premonitions. His gut told him something big was going down, but he couldn't tell if they were included. Shit, he had the ability to search, seek, and find what he needed to know, but with his oath, he closed the one path he could use to find answers to his questions.

At this juncture, he'd placed the shift, if that's what he could call it, in the back of his mind and chose to enjoy the rest of the evening.

****

Shelby unfolded her arms from Kyle. "You didn't, but I think I frightened you." Very strange…The familiar hum of Tim's presence echoed. The comforting sound changed into a horrible staccato rhythm she had never experienced. Her heart paced with the beat. Just as quick, the discordant pitch stopped. Then his spirit left again. Tim's warning and Kyle's response occurred at the same time, were they related? She didn't know and retreated one step.

When she touched Kyle, an unmistakable surreal contact melded their forces together, very close to a spiritual connection. The attraction between them could be attributed to yin and yang, male-female. Shadows don't exist without light, but there was more relevance. She couldn't attach a description to their bond...yet.

"Did you lose your balance or want to tell me something?" His fingers lightly held on to her arm, then slid down to the inside of her wrist, gliding further, tickling her palm.

Her heart rate accelerated, she opened her mouth and gasped. "I've...I named Annie."

"The dog? How did—?"

"Orphaned...Red coat."

He let go and smiled. "Annie, I like it."

She enjoyed his company and his handsome features attracted her too. The tailored western shirt outlined his broad shoulders and molded to each ripple of his sinewy chest. Her gaze marched on to his slim waist and glanced lower. He emitted sex appeal. She reacted like any other woman. Every time he chuckled, her insides twirled, sending erotic flames, building a wild fire she didn't want to put out.

The hissing rockets streamed into the ink black sky, detonated and twinkled down to the earth with phosphorescent colors and a montage of patterns. Shelby joined the cacophony of oohs and ahhs.

Shelby angled toward Kyle. "This is great." She pointed at the ball of red fur. "I can't believe she's sleeping through this."

Kyle closed the space between them and lightly touched her with his arm and shoulder. "Annie has a full belly and she knows we'll keep her safe."

Shelby turned. Their gazes met. Her heart hammered inside her chest. There were two sets of fireworks, one in the sky and one between them.

Boom. The pyrotechnic exploded and the profound sound waves broke the spell. To ease the mind numbing, searing impact of his touch, she mentally scanned over her to-do list. *Damn.* She struggled to collect her thoughts. First, she'd try to figure out who killed Tim and why his spirit disappeared. The doll had to be the connection to his death.

Kyle grinned and amplified his voice over the continual barrage of noise. "This is my favorite part."

Shelby kept her vigil, watching the display, the night sky bright with painted colors. "On the account of it being so beautiful or because it's the climax?" She glanced at Kyle and winced when he smiled at her double entendre.

"They never seem to have enough to satisfy me." She rolled her eyes, clamped her lips together, maybe that would keep her mouth shut.

Kyle chuckled, drifted close, placing his mouth near her ear. "I would have to lie down. My neck would get a crick in it if I had to watch the fireworks like this for very long."

His moist, heated breath danced across her skin sending waves of delight to every nerve ending. She swore they were all connected to her clit. Her eyes closed. Did the fairies spread pixie dust over her? When she opened them and pivoted to face Kyle, his gaze met hers.

He winked, his regard eased into a gentle caress. His intent shifted. Entranced, she sank into the liquid brown depths of his eyes fully aware she'd give herself willingly to him, right now.

Awareness detonated, discharging an electrical

storm within her. Bolts of lightning shattered the involuntary response to breathe. Finally, her lungs expanded and her vertigo disappeared. This nexus between them was mind bending and soul altering.

As though in another world, she sensed rather than saw people shuffling around her. Someone bumped into Kyle and all the fireworks ended.

Protectively, he drew her to his side and led her through the crowd. Kyle guided her to an empty bench. After they sat, Annie maneuvered between their feet and curled underneath them.

Her nerves settled and she listened to the music drifting from across the street. She grinned as the patrons' voices buzzed with the night celebrations high up on a balcony. "This reminds me of Bourbon Street, on a smaller scale of course. People are having fun and enjoying the evening."

Kyle arched his eyebrows. "You've been to Mardi Gras?"

"No, especially not during the celebration. I visited under more sedate times. Mardi Gras is a little wild for me. You?"

Kyle smiled. "Ah, the Big Easy. On several occasions."

For the first time, she noticed his dimples. He had two on each side. Kyle's focus drew her in and held her captive. His gaze radiated an emotion she couldn't quite place. She cleared her throat. "So tell me, what other fun things do you do for entertainment? I know you've been to Mardi Gras and the Fourth of July celebration here in Jackson."

A huge smile lit his face and he laughed out loud. "I've been to a few places over the years. But my favorite place is right here." His baritone carried a warm sound.

"Really, I would never have taken you for a man who lets dust gather on his boots."

"If the dust gets a chance to settle, I'd prefer to be at home. What about you?" He draped his arm along the back of the bench resting his hand near Shelby's shoulder but not touching her.

"I like to get away." Vacations were always fun, but this trip was purely for answers. "Do you do a lot of traveling?"

He crossed his legs. "Yeah, guess I do. That's why I like being at home."

"Me too." Shelby's voice trailed off thinking of her ranch and family. She stopped her woolgathering and rose. "I should call it a night. Thank you for your help with Annie. I enjoyed your company and the lovely evening." Not waiting for an answer, she called, "Annie, time to go."

****

Kyle stood and hoped. "Wait, I'll walk you back to your room."

She bent down and picked up the leash. "You don't have to, thanks." When Shelby straightened, her eyes journeyed from his face down to his chest and then traveled lower to his midsection.

He didn't want her to leave. Her bright smile put sunshine in his drab life. With his extensive travel schedule, he met professional women all the time. Hard and fast rule number one, he never dated them. When he did meet ladies, they usually knew his background and their intentions were clear, they wanted his money, not him.

But Shelby was different. The few hours of making her acquaintance, he had learned she was educated, writing a book, gained strength to continue after losing her husband, and a genuinely gracious woman.

He didn't refute the sexual attraction and wanted her in every way a red-blooded man desired a woman. But there was a difference. He wanted to caress every inch of her with his hands, tongue, and body. From their reactions when they brushed against one another, he discerned their releases would be erotic and on a different level than any he'd ever experienced.

When he saw where Shelby's gaze landed, his heart raced and his ego soared to new heights. Her cheeks blushed to crimson. Blood rushed to his groin. His hustler reacted and he adjusted his jeans. He wouldn't let her wiggle out of the few minutes they had left to share. Plus, he couldn't shake the dark foreboding he had earlier.

Her safety was his responsibility. The guard he had placed at Shelby's room kept him updated via texts. He could delegate the task, but he didn't want to. He wanted to escort her.

She lifted her long, fixed stare to connect with his. He wanted a few more minutes with her. "Dance with me?"

"On the sidewalk?" She rolled her shoulders. "I'd like that." Her lips drifted up at each corner.

He noted her "tells" as a signal for a positive outcome. She wouldn't be good in a poker game. He had to remember, if she ever partnered up with him, make sure she wore sunglasses and loose clothing. Nope, the lift of her mouth would be a dead giveaway.

Patsy Cline's song "Crazy" drifted from the bar. In

several paces, he stood in front of her. He gathered her right hand in his left and the other rested on Shelby's hip, letting her chose the distance between them. As he shifted his weight, she closed the space and laid her cheek against his shoulder. When the music ended, his palm slid to her lower back, holding her responsive body, willing her to continue dancing.

Vince Gill's "Go Rest High on That Mountain" played and she hadn't stepped away. With each sway, she leaned against him in full contact. Pleasure scuttled down from his head to his balls because her position showed trust. Yes, there was a connection. The summer night's breeze wasn't enough to cool the heat of their movement. Shelby's face burrowed into the crook of his neck and her breath skimmed across his skin. The heat glazed his flesh. His heart pounded, raising his temperature. Beads of sweat trickled down his back and he grasped her tighter.

Drops of moisture rolled down his chest. Shelby sniffed, her gaze found his. Tears dripped off her chin and he froze. "Shelby?"

"Sorry...I should go."

He nodded and draped his arm over her shoulder. The sidewalk narrowed, people milled about and he didn't get a chance to talk.

At the hotel, she used her keycard, opened the door and crossed the threshold.

"Let me check your room."

She turned to him. "No, I'm fine. Nice meeting you and thanks again for everything."

"It was my pleasure. You take care, Shelby...what's your last name?"

"Littleton. And yours is Pressley? Did I remember

correctly?"

"Yes, ma'am."

"You too, Kyle Pressley."

"Can I help you with Annie? I could take her home with me tonight and bring her back in the morning?"

"No, she'll be fine. I'll tell the front desk about her tomorrow."

"Then have a good night, Shelby Littleton."

"You too."

He spun and headed toward his bodyguard. "Hey, Sam, thanks for watching."

Sam nodded. "Never seen you like this before."

Kyle kept walking past the man who waited for his response. "What are you talking about?"

Sam caught up to him and smirked. "Son, I've known you since you were a teenager and you're taken with the lady. Don't try and deny it."

Kyle released all the air out of his lungs then filled them again. "I'm interested in getting to know her, that's all."

He wanted to know Shelby Littleton's favorite color, flower, and music. Something about the last song made her cry and he questioned if he'd ever get the chance to ask. Hell, he could come up with a reason...morning coffee and donuts...who could turn down pastries and a caffeine jolt?

Sam waved. "Goodnight, I'm meeting Linda for a late dinner."

"'Night and tell your lovely wife I said hello."

****

Shelby closed the door and sighed. How could a simple phrase, *have a good night Shelby Littleton*, convey so much tenderness? Her stomach fluttered.

When they had touched, explosions the size of Texas blasted through her body and blazed a fiery trail over her skin.

God, she would miss getting to know Kyle better. What was she thinking? She should have reminded him about his offer to be her guide. Instead, she let a perfect opportunity slip out of her grasp. She leaned against the doorjamb. It was probably for the best. Her home was with her family and work, twenty-four hours south of here.

Shelby stroked her arms warding off the chill, her tired muscles begged to be stretched. Wyoming nights were cold and a hot shower would warm her. She focused on the welcoming bed with Annie comfortable on top of the bedspread. "Humpf." She straightened her shoulders and squared them. Tomorrow was a new day and she'd get back to researching her husband's journal entries.

A hum whispered near Shelby. She smiled. Tim would join her in a few seconds. His presence drifted around her. "Hey, sweetheart, why did you leave, do you have a to-do list in your world? No, don't tell me. I won't get the humor, I promise. Listen, we have a lot to talk about, but I'm going to get my shower first."

At last in her nightgown, Tim's company soothed her. Shelby breathed, "I love you and miss you so." She stretched her hands to touch him. The ambient temperature dropped, his spirit skimmed over her fingers, traveled up her arms then enveloped her body. She shivered from the cool air and quivered with anticipation. Her ears popped. "What are you trying to tell me?" She followed the air differential to where he hovered above her backpack. She understood.

On the bed, she carefully unwrapped and held the doll. A vibration coursed through her and an odd aura emanated from Ten-Blue-Sun. "Tim, what's happening?" A pure light encased her while a loving and healing sensation stroked her soul. She relaxed and her heart opened to a world she never knew existed.

A word about the author...

Susan lives on a ranch in Texas with her husband. After work and leaving the dangerous & sizzlin' hot world of her stories, she enjoys skydiving, the great outdoors, and a fine glass of wine from time to time.

Susan enjoys hearing from her readers at Susan@SusanJPOwens.com or visit her website at http://wwwSusanJPOwens.com

Thank you for purchasing
this publication of The Wild Rose Press, Inc.

If you enjoyed the story, we would appreciate
your letting others know by leaving a review.

For other wonderful stories,
please visit our on-line bookstore at
www.thewildrosepress.com.

For questions or more information
contact us at
info@thewildrosepress.com.

The Wild Rose Press, Inc.
www.thewildrosepress.com

Stay current with The Wild Rose Press, Inc.

Like us on Facebook
https://www.facebook.com/TheWildRosePress

And Follow us on Twitter

https://twitter.com/WildRosePress

www.ingramcontent.com/pod-product-compliance
Lightning Source LLC
Chambersburg PA
CBHW071355170626
46811CB00003B/1138